Family Record

ENGLISH TRANSLATIONS OF WORKS BY PATRICK MODIANO

From Yale University Press
After the Circus
Family Record
Little Jewel
Paris Nocturne
Pedigree: A Memoir
Sleep of Memory
Such Fine Boys
Sundays in August
Suspended Sentences: Three Novellas (Afterimage,
    Suspended Sentences, and Flowers of Ruin)

Also available
The Black Notebook
Catherine Certitude
Dora Bruder
Honeymoon
In the Café of Lost Youth
Lacombe, Lucien
Missing Person
The Occupation Trilogy (The Night Watch, Ring Roads,
    and La Place de l'Etoile)
Out of the Dark
So You Don't Get Lost in the Neighborhood
Villa Triste
Young Once

Family Record

PATRICK MODIANO

TRANSLATED FROM THE FRENCH

BY MARK POLIZZOTTI

YALE UNIVERSITY PRESS ■ NEW HAVEN AND LONDON

A MARGELLOS
WORLD REPUBLIC OF LETTERS BOOK

The Margellos World Republic of Letters is dedicated to making literary works from around the globe available in English through translation. It brings to the English-speaking world the work of leading poets, novelists, essayists, philosophers, and playwrights from Europe, Latin America, Africa, Asia, and the Middle East to stimulate international discourse and creative exchange.

Yale University Press books may be purchased in quantity for educational, business, or promotional use. For information, please e-mail sales.press@yale.edu (U.S. office) or sales@yaleup.co.uk (U.K. office).

Set in Electra and Nobel types by Tseng Information Systems, Inc.
Printed in the United States of America.

Library of Congress Control Number: 2018967876
ISBN 978-0-300-23831-0 (paper : alk. paper)

A catalogue record for this book is available from the British Library.

This paper meets the requirements of ANSI/NISO Z39.48-1992 (Permanence of Paper).

10 9 8 7 6 5 4 3 2 1

For Rudy,

For Josée and Henri Bozo

To live is to persist in finishing a memory.

—René Char

Family Record

I was watching my daughter through the glass. She was asleep, resting on her left cheek, mouth hanging open. She was barely two days old and you couldn't see the movement of her breathing.

I pressed my forehead against the pane. Only a few inches separated me from her cradle and I wouldn't have wondered had it floated into the air, weightless. The branch of a plane tree caressed the window with the regularity of a fan blade. My daughter was the only inhabitant of that white and powder-blue room called the Caroline Herrick Nursery. The nurse had pushed the cradle close to the pane so I could see her.

She wasn't moving. An expression of beatitude floated on her tiny face. The branch kept swaying silently. My nose flattened against the glass, leaving a spot of fog.

When the nurse returned, I bolted upright. It was nearly five o'clock and I didn't have a second to lose if I wanted to make it to town hall before the Office of Records closed.

I rushed down the hospital stairs, leafing through a small book with a red leather cover: our "Family Record Book." The title evoked the same respect I feel for all official documents, diplomas, notarized transactions, genealogical charts, zoning ordinances, archival papers, pedigrees . . . On the first two pages was a copy of my marriage certificate, with my full name and that of my wife. We had left blank the lines for "son of," to avoid the morass of my civil status. The fact is, I don't know where I was born or what names my parents were using at the time. A navy-blue piece of paper, folded in four, was stapled to this family record: my parents' marriage certificate. My father appears under an assumed name because the wedding had taken place during the Occupation. It said:

FRENCH STATE

Haute-Savoie Department

Megève, Office of the Mayor

On 24 February Nineteen Hundred Forty-four, at five-thirty p.m.

The following persons publicly appeared before us in the Town Hall:

Guy Jaspaard de Jonghe, and

Maria Luisa C.

The intended spouses have each declared that they wish to live as man and wife and we have pronounced by the powers vested in us that they are hereby united by the bonds of matrimony.

What were my father and mother doing in Megève in February 1944? I would know soon enough—I thought. And what about this "de Jonghe" that my father had appended to his initial borrowed name? De Jonghe. That's him all over.

I noticed Koromindé's car parked on the street about a dozen yards from the hospital entrance. He was behind the wheel, engrossed in a magazine. He raised his eyes and smiled at me.

I had met him the night before in a restaurant with vaguely Basque décor. It was located near Porte de Bagatelle, one of those places you find yourself in when something important has happened, a place you would never go under normal circumstances. My daughter was born at 9 p.m. I had seen her before she was taken into the nursery, kissed her sleeping mother. Outside, I had wandered aimlessly down the empty streets of Neuilly, beneath the autumn rain. Midnight. I was the last diner in this restaurant, where a man I could see only from behind stood leaning against the bar. The telephone rang and the bartender answered. He turned to the man:

"Monsieur Koromindé, it's for you."

Koromindé . . . The name of one of my father's friends in his youth, who often came to the house when I was little. He took the phone and I recognized his deep, gentle voice, the way he rolled his r's. He hung up. I stood and walked over to him.

"Are you Jean Koromindé?"

"I am."

He stared at me in surprise. I introduced myself. He let out an exclamation. Then, with a sad smile:

"You've grown . . ."

"Yes," I answered, hunching over as if in apology. I told him the news that I was a father, as of several hours ago. He seemed moved and bought me a drink to celebrate the birth of my child.

"Becoming a father is something, isn't it?"

"Yes."

We left the restaurant together. It was called the Esperia.

Koromindé offered to drive me home and opened the passenger door of an old black Régence. During the ride, we talked about my father. It had been twenty years since he'd last seen him. It had been ten since I'd had any word from him. Neither of us knew what had become of him. Koromindé remembered an evening in 1942 when he and my father had dinner together, at the Esperia, in fact . . . And it was there, in that very same restaurant, on an evening thirty years later, that he learned about the birth of "the little girl."

"How time flies."

His eyes were misting up.

"And that little girl of yours, do I get to meet her?"

That's when I offered to have him drive me to the town hall the next day, when I would register my daughter. He was thrilled. We agreed to meet in front of the hospital at five o'clock sharp.

In daylight, his car looked even more dilapidated than the night before. He stuffed the magazine he'd been reading into a jacket pocket and opened the door for me. He was wearing shades with heavy frames and bluish lenses.

"We don't have much time," I said. "The Office of Records closes at five-thirty."

He looked at his watch:

"Not to worry."

He drove slowly, serenely.

"Do you think I've changed a lot in twenty years?"

I closed my eyes to recapture the image I had of him at that time: an energetic blond who constantly ran his index finger over his mustache, spoke in short, staccato sentences, and laughed a great deal. Always dressed in light-colored suits. That was how he hovered over my memories of childhood.

"I've aged, haven't I?"

He had. His face had narrowed and his skin had acquired a grayish cast. He had lost his beautiful blond hair.

"Not really," I said.

He worked the stick shift and turned the steering wheel with generous, lazy movements. As he veered onto an avenue perpendicular to the one the hospital was on, he made too wide a turn and the Régence hit the curb. He shrugged.

"I wonder if your father still looks like Rhett Butler . . . you know . . . *Gone with the Wind.*"

"So do I."

"I'm his oldest friend . . . We've known each other since we were ten, back in Cité d'Hauteville . . ."

He drove down the middle of the avenue and scraped against a truck. Then he turned on the radio with a mechanical gesture. Someone was talking about the economic situation, which according to him was growing worse and worse. He predicted a crash as dire as the one in 1929. I thought about the blue-and-white room in which my daughter was asleep and the swaying plane branch that caressed the window.

Koromindé stopped at a red light. He was lost in thought. The lights changed three times and he didn't move. He remained expressionless behind his tinted glasses. Finally, he asked:

"So does your daughter look like him?"

What could I say? Maybe *he* knew what my father and mother had been doing in Megève in February 1944 and how they had celebrated their peculiar wedding. I didn't want to ask him quite yet, for fear of distracting him even more and causing an accident.

We followed Boulevard d'Inkermann at parade speed. He pointed out a sand-colored building on the right with porthole windows and large semicircular balconies.

"Your father lived there for a month . . . on the top floor . . ."

He might even have celebrated his twenty-fifth birthday there, but Koromindé wasn't sure: all the buildings where my father had lived, he said, had the same basic façade. That's how it was. He hadn't forgotten that late afternoon in the summer of '37 and the terrace that the last rays of sunlight bathed in rosy orange. My father, it seemed, greeted his guests bare-chested, in a bathrobe. In the middle of the sidewalk, he had set up an old sofa and some lawn chairs.

"And I served the drinks."

Crossing Boulevard Bineau, he ran a red light and narrowly missed another car, but he didn't care. He turned left onto Rue Borghese. Where did Rue Borghese lead? I looked at my watch. Five twenty-one. The Office of Records was about to close. I was seized by panic. What if they refused to register my daughter? I opened the glove compartment, thinking I might find a street map of Paris and environs.

"Are you sure this is the right way?" I asked Koromindé.

"I don't think it is."

He started to make a U-turn—but no, better to keep going straight. We returned to Boulevard Victor-Hugo, then Boulevard d'Inkermann. Now Koromindé had the pedal floored. Beads of sweat were running down his temples. He too looked at his watch. He murmured, in a toneless voice:

"I swear to you, my boy, we'll make it in time."

He ran another red light. I shut my eyes. He sped faster and gave short, sharp honks on the horn. The old Régence was shaking. We arrived at Avenue du Roule. In front of the church, the car stalled.

We left the Régence and speed-walked toward the town hall, two hundred yards farther down the avenue. Koromindé was limping slightly and I was in front. I started to run. Koromindé did too, but his left leg dragged and soon I was well ahead of him. I turned around: he was waving his arm in distress, but I kept running faster and faster. Koromindé, discouraged, slowed down. He mopped his brow and temples with a navy-blue handkerchief. Bounding up the steps of the town hall, I gestured at him frantically. He managed to join me, so out of breath that he couldn't make a sound. I grabbed him by the wrist and we crossed the foyer, where a sign said "Office of Records — 2nd floor, left." Koromindé was deathly pale. I thought he was about to go into cardiac arrest and I propped him up as we climbed the stairs. I pushed open the door to the Office of Records with my shoulder, while my two hands supported Koromindé. He stumbled and his weight dragged me down with him. We slipped and fell backward in the middle of the room, and the registry employees gaped at us from behind the bars of their counter.

I got up first and headed for the counter, clearing my throat. Koromindé collapsed onto a bench in the back of the room.

There were three of them: two women in blouses, fifties, harsh, nervous, bobbed slate-colored hair, who looked like twins; and a tall man with a thick waxed mustache.

"Can I help you?" one of the women said.

Her tone was at once intimidated and threatening.

"I'm here for a birth registration."

"You sure took your time," the other woman said, without warmth.

The man squinted at me. Our sudden appearance had made a rather poor impression.

"Tell them we very truthfully regret this delay," Koromindé whispered from the back of the room.

You could tell from that "very truthfully" that French was not his native tongue. He limped up to me. One of the women slid a sheet of paper toward us under the bars of her window and said in a perfidious voice:

"Fill out the form."

I patted my pockets in search of a pen, then turned toward Koromindé. He handed me a pencil.

"No pencil," hissed the fellow in the mustache.

The three of them stood behind the bars, watching us in silence.

"You wouldn't have a pen . . . by any chance?" I asked.

Mr. Mustache looked stupefied. The twin sisters folded their arms over their chests.

"Please, sir, a pen," Koromindé repeated in a plaintive voice.

The man with the mustache pushed a green ballpoint through the bars. Koromindé thanked him. The twins kept their arms folded in disapproval.

Koromindé handed me the ballpoint and I began filling out the form, using the information in the Family Record Book to guide me. I wanted my daughter to be named Zénaïde, perhaps in memory of Zénaïde Rachevski, a stunning woman who had captivated me as a child. Koromindé was looking over my shoulder to oversee what I was writing.

When I had finished, Koromindé took the sheet and read it, knitting his brow. Then he handed it to one of the twins.

"This isn't on the list of French names," she said, stabbing her finger on "Zénaïde," which I had spelled out in huge capitals.

"And what of it, madam?" asked Koromindé, in an altered voice.

"You cannot give a child this name."

The other twin had bent her head near her sister's and their foreheads met. I was crushed.

"So what can we do?" asked Koromindé.

She picked up the phone and dialed a two-digit number.

She asked if the first name "Zénaïde" was "on the list." The answer was: NO.

"You cannot give a child this name."

I swayed on my feet, my throat tightening.

The man with the mustache approached in turn and picked up the form.

"But of course we can, miss," Koromindé whispered, as if giving away a secret. "We can give the child this name."

And he raised his hand, very slowly, like a benediction.

"It was his godmother's name."

The man with the mustache bent forward and leaned his ramlike forehead against the bars.

"In that case, gentlemen, it is a special situation, and an entirely different matter."

He had an unctuous voice that did not at all match his bearing.

"Certain names are handed down in families, and however peculiar they might be, we have no quarrel with them. None whatsoever."

He molded his sentences and every word that emerged from his mouth was coated in Vaseline.

"Let us go with Zénaïde!"

"Thank you, sir, thank you!"

He made a sign of exasperation in the direction of the twin sisters and executed a pirouette before disappearing, like a dancer. We heard someone typing in the rear office. Koromindé and I weren't quite sure whether we should wait. The two twins sorted through a stack of papers, talking in very low murmurs.

"A lot of births today, ladies? Business good?" Koromindé asked, as if trying to ingratiate himself.

No reply. I lit a cigarette, offered the pack to Koromindé, then to the two women.

"Would you like a cigarette?"

But they pretended not to hear me.

Finally, the man with the mustache stuck his head through the opening of a side door and said:

"This way, please."

We found ourselves on the other side of the barred windows, where the two sisters and the man with the mustache officiated. The latter signaled for us to go into the rear office. The twins kept churning mechanically through their stacks of paperwork.

A small corner office, its two windows looking out onto the street. Empty walls, the color of a Havana cigar. A dark wooden desk with many drawers, on top of which lay an open register.

"Gentlemen, if you would please read and sign."

The text, typed without a single error, specified that a child of female sex, named Zénaïde, was born at nine o'clock on the evening of October 22 of that year . . . A dozen lines for which an entire page of the register had been reserved. And the same information on the following page.

"The duplicate."

This time, he handed me a huge fountain pen with a gold cap.

"Have you read it over? No mistakes?" he asked.

"None," I answered.

"None," Koromindé echoed.

I took the pen and slowly, in a large, jagged hand, at the bottom of the two pages, I wrote my first and last names.

Then it was Koromindé's turn. He removed his tinted glasses. A bandage held his right eyelid open, making him look like a lost boxer. He signed, his handwriting even shakier than mine: Jean Koromindé.

"Are you a friend of the family?" asked the man with the mustache.

"A friend of the grandfather's."

One day, in twenty years' time, if she was curious enough to look up this registration—but why would she?—Zénaïde, seeing this signature, would wonder who this Jean Koromindé could have been.

"There, all's well that ends well," the man with the mustache said kindly.

He looked at me with eyes that were gentle, almost paternal, and that even seemed slightly teary. He held out a timid hand and we each shook it in turn. And I then understood why he wore that mustache. Without it, his features would have collapsed and he would surely have lost the authority required of a civil functionary.

He opened a door.

"You can exit by this stairway," he said in a conspiratorial voice, as if he were showing us a secret passage. "Good-bye, gentlemen. And best of luck. Best of luck . . ."

On the town hall's front steps, we felt funny. There—we had seen to an important formality, and it had gone smoothly. Night was falling. We had to get the Régence running again. We found a mechanic who determined that the car needed a serious repair. Koromindé would come pick it up the next day. We decided to head back to Paris on foot.

We took Avenue du Roule. Koromindé, no longer dragging his leg behind him, walked with a lively step. I couldn't help thinking about the large register book open on the desk. So that's what a civil status register looked like. We must have been thinking the same thing, as Koromindé said:

"Did you see that? It's a funny thing, a civil status register, don't you think?"

And what about him? Had he been registered at some hall of records? What was his original nationality? Belgian? German? Baltic? Russian, probably. And my father, before he called himself "Jaspaard" and appended "de Jonghe" to his name? And my mother? And all the others? And myself? Somewhere there must have existed registers with yellowed pages, where our names and dates of birth, and the names of our parents, were written in India ink, in an ornate hand. But where could these registers be found?

Korominde was whistling next to me. His coat pocket was distended by the magazine he had been reading in the car, whose title I could see in red letters: a popular electronics periodical. Once more, I was tempted to ask him what my father and mother had been doing in Megève in February 1944. But did he even know? After thirty years, memories . . . We had reached the end of Avenue du Roule. It was dark and the dead leaves, coated in mud by the rain, stuck to our heels. Now and again, Korominde scraped the soles of his shoes on the curb. I watched for passing cars, looking for a free taxi. But no, all in all, might as well keep walking.

We entered Avenue de la Porte-des-Ternes, in that neighborhood they had disemboweled to build the Périphérique. A no-man's-land between Maillot and Champerret, devastated, unrecognizable, as if after a bombardment.

"One time I came here with your father," Korominde said.

"Is that so?"

Yes, my father had driven with him around here. He was looking for a garage mechanic who could get a replacement part for his Ford. He didn't remember the exact address, and for some time he and Korominde had crisscrossed the neighborhood, which was now completely demolished. Streets lined with trees whose branches formed a vault. On each side, garages and sheds that looked abandoned. And the sweetish odor of gasoline. Finally, they had stopped in front of an establishment, a supplier of "American parts." Avenue de la Porte-de-Villiers looked like a strip mall in a tiny southwestern town, with its four rows of plane trees. They had sat on a bench and waited for the mechanic to finish the repairs. A German shepherd was stretched out on the sidewalk, asleep. Children chased one another around the middle of the empty avenue, amid dapples of sunlight. It was a Saturday afternoon in August, right after the war. They kept silent. Apparently my father was in a melancholy mood. As for Koromindé, he understood that the time of their youth had ended.

We arrived at Avenue des Ternes and Koromindé started limping again. I took his arm. The streetlamps turned on along Boulevard Gouvion-Saint-Cyr. It was the hour of long lines of cars, jostling crowds, but none of that penetrated the nursery. I again saw the branch calmly swaying against the window.

We had just participated in the beginning of something. That little girl would in some way be our delegate to the future. And on her very first try, she had obtained the mysterious possession that had always eluded us: a civil status.

II

At what point in my life did I meet Henri Marignan? Oh, I couldn't have been twenty at the time. I think of him often. Sometimes he seems to have been one of my father's multiple incarnations. I don't know what became of him. Our first meeting? It occurred at the back of a narrow, coral-red bar on Boulevard des Capucines, the Hole in the Wall. We were the last patrons. Marignan, sitting at a table next to mine, ordered a "rice whiskey," and after taking a sip he said to the bartender:

"It doesn't taste like it did in China."

So I asked him point-blank:

"Do you know China?"

We chatted until four in the morning. About China, naturally, where Marignan had lived for a while before the war. He could still sketch a detailed map of Shanghai on a napkin, and that evening he did one for me. I wanted to know what chances a Westerner had, these days, of entering that enigmatic country and exploring it freely. He hesitated slightly, then pronounced in a solemn voice:

"I believe it's possible."

He stared at me steadily.

"Would you like to try it with me?"

"Of course," I said.

From that moment on, we saw each other daily.

Marignan was over sixty, but looked twenty years younger. Tall, with square shoulders, he wore his hair in a brush-cut. There was no trace of puffiness in his face. The smooth line of his eyebrows, nose, and chin impressed me. Sometimes an expression of helplessness shot through his blue eyes. He always wore double-breasted suits and evidently had a predilection for shoes with very elastic crepe soles that gave him a supple gait.

After a while, I learned who I was dealing with. The information didn't come from him, since he spoke of his past only when asked a direct question.

At twenty-six, he had been sent to Shanghai by a news agency. He started a daily paper that was published in two editions, French and Chinese. He was sought after as an adviser to the Ministry of Communications under Chiang Kai-shek, and there were rumors that Madame Chiang had succumbed to the charms of Henri Marignan. He had remained in China for seven years.

Back in France, he had published a memoir, *Lost Shanghai*, of which I can recite entire pages by heart. In it, he depicts the China of the thirties, with its proliferation of real and fake generals, its bankers, its funeral processions that roam the streets while playing "Viens Poupoule," its thirteen-year-old chanteuses with their shrill voices and pink stockings embroidered with huge yellow butterflies, its stink of opium and rot, and the humid night air that coats shoes and clothing in fungus. The book renders a vibrant and nostalgic homage to Shanghai, the city of his youth. In the years that followed, spurred on by his love of intrigue, he frequented both the Communist International Brigades and the fascist Cagoule. From 1940 to 1945, he undertook mysterious "missions" between Paris, Vichy, and Lisbon. He dropped out of sight, officially speaking, in Berlin, in April 1945. That was Henri Marignan.

I would go see him on Avenue de New York, at number 52, I think, one of the last buildings before the Trocadéro gardens. The apartment belonged to a certain Geneviève Catelain, a refined, vaporous blonde, whose eyes gave off glints of emerald. Sitting with him on the living room sofa, she would say to him when I entered:

"Here's Monsieur Modiano, your accomplice."

More than once, he arranged to see me on Avenue de New York

at around 10 p.m., and each time, there were others in the living room, as if for a celebration or cocktail party. Geneviève Catelain flitted from group to group; Marignan kept to himself. As soon as he saw me, he came forward, stiff-chested and with a bounding step.

"Let's go get some air," he would say.

We wandered aimlessly through Paris. One evening, he showed me the Chinese quarter around the Gare de Lyon, near Avenue Daumesnil. The Arabs had supplanted the Chinese, but there still remained, in Passage Gatbois, a hotel with a sign saying Red Dragon. A "Chinese" restaurant occupied the ground floor. We went upstairs. A large room with walls covered in quilted burgundy velvet, some of it in tatters. A single bulb lit the three dirty windows and gray parquet floor. Some slats were missing. In a corner were piled-up chairs, a trunk, and an old sideboard. The place served as a junk room.

"It's falling apart," Marignan sighed.

He explained that during the Occupation, it was the only opium den in Paris. He had gone there one evening with the actress Luisa Ferida.

Sometimes we would make a detour to the Pagode on Rue de Babylone, or stop in front of that large Chinese house on Rue de Courcelles, on which a plaque stated that it had been built in 1928 by a certain Fernand Bloch. We wandered through the galleries of the Guimet and Cernuschi museums and went for walks in Boulogne, in the Asian gardens of Albert Kahn. Marignan was lost in thought.

I walked him back to Avenue de New York and tried to find out what bound him to the enigmatic Geneviève Catelain.

"A very, very old romance," he confided one evening. "From back when I still officially existed and wasn't the ghost I am today. You know I died in '45, right?"

How had he managed to survive and not be recognized? He said that people's looks change after age forty, and that he had earned a little money writing children's stories under the pseudonym Uncle Ronnie. He wrote them in English, and "Uncle Ronnie's Stories" sold in Great Britain and even the United States. He also did a little art dealing on the side.

But the plan of leaving for China preoccupied him. In the middle of the street, he would suddenly ask:

"Do you think you'll be able to stand the climate?"

Or:

"Are you prepared to spend a year there?"

Or:

"Have you been vaccinated for diphtheria, Patrick?"

Finally, he let me in on his plan. For the past several years, he had been clipping newspaper and magazine photos of Premier Chou En-lai and his entourage, taken at diplomatic banquets or welcoming ceremonies for foreign dignitaries. He had repeatedly watched the newsreels from when the American president visited China. Standing to the left of Chou En-lai, so close that their shoulders touched, was always the same smiling man. And that man was someone Marignan was certain he had known back in Shanghai.

His words came faster and faster, and he looked totally absorbed, as if trying to recapture the contours of a lost world. On Avenue Joffre, in the French Concession, there's a restaurant called Kachenko. Tables covered with sky-blue tablecloths, each holding a small lamp with a green shade. The French consul often goes there. And also Kenneth Cummings, the richest stockbroker in Shanghai. You walk down a few steps to the dance floor. During dinner, the band plays soft music. The musicians are all European, except for the pianist, who's Chinese and doesn't look more than eighteen. It was that pianist—Marignan would have staked his life on it—that we now saw next to Chou En-lai. Back then, he went by the name of Roger Fuseng. He spoke fluent French because he'd been schooled by Jesuits. Marignan considered him his best friend. Roger Fu worked for the newspaper and wrote articles in Chinese, or else served as translator. He played in the band at the Kachenko until midnight, and Marignan would go see him every evening. Fu was twenty-five and a stunning boy. He liked to hang out. Nights at the Casanova on Avenue Edward VII and at the Ritz on Rue Chu-Pao-San, among the Chinese taxi girls and the White Russians from Harbin . . . Roger Fu-seng always ended up sitting at the piano and plunking out a tune by Cole Porter. For Marignan, Fu was the Shanghai of that time.

He had to get back in touch with him, come what may, now that he had become a familiar of Chou En-lai. Marignan had been thinking about it for years, but each time, the difficulty of the enterprise had made him give up. He was glad to have met a "youngster" like me who could spur him on. And indeed, I'm used to listening to people, to sharing their dreams and encouraging them in their grand plans.

Several weeks passed and Marignan kept making phone calls in the cafés where we would meet. He never said anything to me, and when I dared ask, he invariably answered:

"We'll find the 'angle.'"

One afternoon, he asked me to come see him on Avenue de New York. He opened the door to the apartment and pulled me into the living room. We found ourselves alone in the middle of that vast white room whose four French windows looked out on the Seine. There were more vases of flowers than usual. Bouquets of orchids, roses, and irises, and in back, a small orange tree.

He offered me one of the gold-tipped cigarettes that Geneviève Catelain smoked and laid out the situation. As he saw it, there was only one path to reestablishing contact with Roger Fu-seng: the embassy of the People's Republic of China in Paris. He just had to meet a member of the embassy — however minor — and confide in him candidly. Marignan felt that his relatively good command of the Chinese language would work in our favor. Now, it was very difficult to gain access to the diplomatic personnel on Avenue George-V. Surely there were ties between France and China, trade associations, some sort of Franco-Chinese exchange group. But how did one penetrate such circles? And so, he had thought of George Wo-heu, a subtle, slinky young man who had worked at the Shanghai Commerce and Savings Bank when they were young and obtained funds for him from various backers with which to start his newspaper. Wo-heu had settled in Paris some thirty years ago and was now a diamond merchant.

We waited for him to arrive.

He glided toward us, rolling on invisible skates. Marignan introduced us and Wo-heu favored me with a smile that split his face up to his temples. Though short and plump, he seemed quite supple. He had a moonlike countenance and brushed-back silver hair. His dark gray pinstripe suit was perfectly tailored. He sat on the sofa, rubbing together hands with varnished nails.

"So, Toto?" he shot at Marignan.

The latter cleared his throat.

"What's new, Toto?" His voice was melodious.

Without further ado, Marignan told him we were planning a trip to China and that we had to make contact as soon as possible with the embassy of the People's Republic of China. Would he have an "in"?

He burst out in a laugh that split his face almost to the forehead.

"And that's why you asked me here?"

He pulled a cigarette from a leather case, which he closed with a nervous motion. He settled back into the sofa. There before us, smooth and chubby, he looked like he'd just stepped out of a scented bath. Moreover, he smelled of Penhaligon's.

He suddenly became serious. He knit his brow.

"Well, actually, yes, I do know people at the Chinese embassy, Toto. Only . . . only . . ." And he suspended his sentence, as if to keep us waiting. "Only, it's going to be very difficult to talk to them about you . . ."

I was surprised Marignan didn't bring up Roger Fu-seng, but he must have had his reasons.

"I'd only need to see some kind of undersecretary," Marignan said.

Wo-heu didn't inhale and pushed the smoke out in a single breath. Each time, a compact cloud masked his face.

"Naturally," he said. "Only, the People's Republic of China bears no relation to the China we used to know. You understand, my dear Toto?"

"Yes . . ." said Marignan.

"I have connections with a commercial attaché," Wo-heu said, looking toward the windows and the rear of the room, as if tracing the path of a butterfly. "But why do you want to go back there?"

Marignan didn't answer.

"You won't recognize any of it, dear Toto."

Shadows slowly invaded the room. Marignan didn't turn on the lights. The two of them had fallen silent. George Wo-heu closed his eyes. Marignan had a wrinkle that cut across his right cheek. The sound of a door opening and closing. A pastel silhouette. Geneviève Catelain.

"Why are you in the dark?" she asked.

Wo-heu leapt up and kissed her hand.

"George Wo. What a lovely surprise . . ."

We walked Wo to a taxi stand on Avenue d'Iéna.

"I'll call you," he said to us. "Be patient. Be very patient."

Marignan and I felt as if we had taken a crucial step forward.

We waited for George Wo-heu's phone calls on Avenue de New York, in Marignan's room. You reached it by climbing a small stairway that angled off from the apartment's vestibule. On the nightstand was a photo of Geneviève Catelain at twenty, face smooth and eyes brighter than usual. She was wearing an aviator's helmet from which escaped one lock of blond hair. Marignan told me she used to break world records in "ridiculous old rattletraps." I was in love with her.

George Wo-heu called in the evenings, anywhere from seven to ten. To allay our anxiety and impatience, Marignan dictated his notes to me, while consulting an old Shanghai phone book.

C. T. WANG, 90 Rue Amiral-Courbet, 09-12-14
BETH-EL JEWISH SYNAGOGUE, 24 Foochow Road
D. HARDIVILLIERS, 2 Bubbling Well Road, 07-09-01
VENUS, 3 Szechuen Road, 10-41-62
D'AUXION DE RUFFÉ, 20 Zeng wou Tseng, 01-41-28
ÉTABLISSEMENTS SASSOON, Soochow Creek, 78-20-11
SINCÈRE DEPARTMENT STORES, Nanking Road, 40-33-17

A spindly ring. We didn't answer until we were sure it was the telephone. Marignan picked up the receiver, and I the extension. The exchanges were always the same:

"Hello? George Wo?" Marignan said in a flat voice.

"How are you, Henri?"

"Fine. And you?"

A few seconds of silence.

"So what's new, Wo?" Marignan asked in a falsely jovial tone.

"I'm making contacts."

"And?"

"It's coming along, my dear Toto. Just a little more patience."

"For how long, George?"

"I'll call you. So long, Henri."

"So long, Wo."

He hung up. And each time, we were sorely disappointed.

From the large living room came the buzz of conversation. They had company, as usual. Geneviève Catelain waved us over. We walked toward her through small clusters of guests, but didn't speak to anyone. She saw us to the door.

"See you later, Henri," she said to Marignan. "Don't be home too late."

She stood in the doorway, blonde and charged with a mysterious electricity that moved me.

The night began. Often we would meet up with George Wo-heu and the three of us would have dinner at the Calavados, a throwback restaurant on Avenue Pierre-1er-de-Serbie, staying out until two in the morning. The ordeal left us feeling edgy. There was no use asking him directly about what contacts he might or might not have made at the embassy on our behalf. He avoided answering by changing the subject, or by uttering generalities such as, "Embassies are like rabbits. You have to approach them slowly so as not to scare them off, right, Toto?" His smile split his face in two. Marignan never attacked frontally, instead proceeding by sly allusions and subtle asides. George Wo-heu dodged them all. Worn out, Marignan would end up asking, "Do you really think we'll get to meet someone at the embassy?" To which George Wo-heu invariably replied, "You know perfectly well that China is a long patience, my dear Toto, and you have to deserve her." He drew on his cigarette, immediately exhaled, and his face disappeared behind a screen of smoke.

Before taking his leave, he would say:

"I'll call you tomorrow. I might have news. So long."

Then Marignan and I, to build up our hope and morale, would have a last drink in the empty room of the Calavados. What would Roger Fu-seng's reaction be when he learned that his old friend Henri, from the *Journal de Shanghai*, was trying to find him? He couldn't have forgotten. Not possible.

Diplomatic relations would soon be established between France and China, across the miles and the years. But Wo-heu was surely right and it was important not to rush things. We might snap the gossamer thread.

On Avenue de New York, at the door to his building, Marignan shook hands good-bye.

"Not a word about this China business to Geneviève, okay, old man? I'm counting on you. See you tomorrow. Don't worry—the end is in sight."

I returned to my tiny room on Square de Graisivaudan. I leaned on the windowsill. Why did Marignan want to go to China? In hopes of recapturing his youth, I told myself. And what about me? It was the other side of the world. I convinced myself that it was where I would find my roots, my home, my native soil, everything I didn't have.

The telephone rang and, despite our intercessor's promises, there was never any news. We now spent our days waiting in a café on Avenue de New York, next door to the apartment. George Wo-heu would come join us.

Marignan knocked back strong, sugary drinks, and I let myself follow suit. At sixty, he seemed to hold his liquor much better than I could. He was from the provinces, and his physique still retained that peasant robustness and solidity. Except his eyes, of course, which betrayed an inner collapse.

He spoke to me of the lotus fields in Suchow. Very early in the morning, we would cross the lake in a boat and see the lotus flowers open with the sunrise.

The days went by. We hardly ever left the café. We let ourselves be overcome by a kind of despondency. We still experienced moments of hope and elation, the certainty that we would be leaving soon. But the seasons changed. Soon there was nothing around us but a tender fog, pierced by the ever hazier contour of George Wo.

III

Rue Léon-Vaudoyer and a few other small streets that all looked
the same formed a vague enclave between two parts of the 7th arrondissement. On the right began the aristocratic part of the seventh; to
the left was Grenelle, the Ecole Militaire, and, back when, the din of
rowdy soldiers in the brasseries of La Motte-Picquet.

My grandmother lived on that Rue Léon-Vaudoyer. When? In
the thirties, I believe. At what address? I don't know, but the buildings on Rue Léon-Vaudoyer were all built on the same model around
1900, such that the same entryways, the same windows, the same
corbeling form a monotonous façade stretching from one end of the
street to the other on both sides. In the gap between them, you can
see the Eiffel Tower. On the first house on the right, a plaque states:
"Property of Les Rentiers de l'Avenir." Perhaps she lived there. I know
almost nothing about her. I don't know what she looked like, as every
photograph of her — assuming there were any — has vanished. She was
the daughter of an upholsterer from Philadelphia. My grandfather, for
his part, had spent part of his youth in Alexandria, before leaving for
Venezuela. By what twists of fate had they met in Paris, and had she
ended up spending her final years on Rue Léon-Vaudoyer?

I followed the path she must have taken to return home. It was
a sunny October afternoon. I walked up all the neighboring streets:
Rue César-Franck, Rue Albert-de-Lapparent, Rue José-Marie-de-
Heredia . . . In what shops had she been a regular customer? There's
a grocery store on Rue César-Franck. Was it already there at the time?
On Rue Valentin-Haüy, an old restaurant still bears the inscription

in a semicircular arch: "Wines and spirits." Did her two sons take her there one evening?

I entered Rue Léon-Vaudoyer, first from Avenue de Saxe, then via Rue Pérignon, stopping in front of each building entrance. In each stairwell were identical elevators, and among them was the one she used to take. She knew peaceful late afternoons like this one, when she came home under the same sun and along the same sidewalk. And one could forget about the looming war.

At the corner of Avenue de Saxe, I glanced back one final time at Rue Léon-Vaudoyer. A charmless, treeless street, just like dozens of others on the fringes of Paris's bourgeois neighborhoods. Nearby, on Avenue de Saxe, I went into an old bookstore. Did she sometimes go there to buy a novel? No, the bookseller told me she'd been in that location for only fifteen years, and before that the space was a hat shop. Stores change ownership: that's business. You end up not really knowing the exact space that things occupied. Thus, in 1917, when Big Bertha threatened Paris, my grandmother had brought her children to a place near Enghien, to a relative of hers, a certain James Levy. They came for him one day and no one ever saw him again. My grandmother wrote to the police and the Army Ministry. To no avail. She finally decided they had shot James Levy by mistake, as a German spy.

I, too, wanted to know more, but I've yet to find the slightest trace, the slightest proof of James Levy's existence on Earth. I even consulted archives in the Enghien town hall. And anyway, was it near Enghien?

IV

At age eighteen, my mother embarked on a film career in her native city of Antwerp. Before that, she had worked for the gas company and taken elocution lessons, but when they built a studio on Pyckestraat, the initiative of a certain Jan Vanderheyden, she showed up and was hired.

A group quickly formed around Vanderheyden, who always employed the same cast and crew. He served as both producer and director and shot his movies in record time. The Pyckestraat studio was such a hive of activity that the papers called it "De Antwerpche Hollywood": the Hollywood of Antwerp.

My mother was the very young star of four Vanderheyden films. He shot the first two—*This Man Is an Angel* and *Janssens versus Peeters*—in the year 1939. The next two, *Janssens and Peeters Reconciled* and *Good Luck, Monika*, are from 1941. Three of these movies were light comedies set in Antwerp that make Vanderheyden (as one reviewer said) a kind of Belgian Marcel Pagnol; the fourth, *Monika*, was a musical.

Meantime, Vanderheyden's production company had been placed under German control and my mother was sent to Berlin for several weeks, where she had a minor role in Willi Forst's *Bel Ami*.

That year, 1939, she also signed with the Empire Theater in Antwerp. She worked as a "showgirl" and a "model." From June through December, the Empire staged an adaptation of *No, No, Nanette*, and my mother was in it. Then, as of January 1940, she appeared in a "current events" variety show called *Tomorrow Will Be Better*. She was the centerpiece of the final tableau. While the chorus girls danced with "Chamberlain" umbrellas, my mother rose up in a basket, golden rays crowning her head. Higher and higher she rose, the rain stopped, the umbrellas came down. She was the image of the rising sun, its light dissipating all the shadows of the year 1940. From up in her basket, my mother waved to the audience and the orchestra played a medley. The curtain fell. And each time, for a laugh, the stagehands would leave her in the basket, alone up there in the dark.

She lived on the second floor of a small house near Quai Van Dyck. One of her windows looked out on the Scheldt and the promenade along its banks, with the large café at the end. The Empire Theater and its dressing room, where every evening she applied her makeup. The Customs House. The waterfront area with its port and docks. I see her crossing the avenue as a streetcar rattles by, its yellow light swallowed by the fog. It's nighttime. You can hear the horns of the steamers.

The Empire's wardrobe master was fond of my mother and offered to become her manager. A chubby-cheeked man with horn-rimmed glasses, who spoke very slowly. But at night, in a sailors' bar in the Greek quarter, he performed a song-and-dance routine dressed as Madame Butterfly. According to him, Vanderheyden's films, charming and frequent as they might be, were not enough to sustain an actress's career. Have to aim higher, my dear. And in fact, he knew some big-time producers who were about to make a film but still needed a girl for the supporting role. He brought my mother to meet them.

The producers were a certain Felix Openfeld and his father, whom everyone called Openfeld Senior. The latter, a gemstone dealer in Berlin, had fled to Antwerp when Hitler seized power in Germany and Jewish-owned businesses came under threat. The son had been production manager for the German film company Terra-Film, then worked in the United States.

They liked my mother. They didn't even give her a screen test, but instead had her act out a scene from the script right then and there. It was called *Swimmers and Detectives*, and had been custom-written for the Dutch Olympic swimming champion Wily den Ouden, who wanted to get her start in the movies. From what my mother said, the rather thin mystery plot was mainly an excuse for diving and synchronized swimming scenes. My mother played Wily den Ouden's best friend.

I found the contract she signed at the time. Two pages on heavy, watermarked, sky-blue paper, with the letterhead of Openfeld Films. The O of Openfeld is very large, with an elegant loop, upstrokes and downstrokes. Inside the O, a miniature Brandenburg Gate, finely rendered. I suppose it was there to remind people of the two producers' Berlin origins.

The contract stated that my future mother would receive an advance of seventy-five thousand Belgian francs, payable in installments at the start of each week of shooting. Both parties agreed that this salary could not be increased or reduced unless the contract was terminated or extended, as the case may be. It also stipulated that time spent in makeup and dressing would be considered preparation time and not billable hours.

At the bottom of the page, my mother's diligent signature. Felix Openfeld's hasty signature. And a third, even more jagged, under which someone typed "Mr. Openfeld Senior."

The contract is dated April 21, 1940.

They took my mother to dinner that evening. The wardrobe manager was among the party, as was the screenwriter, Henri Putmann, whose nationality was a mystery: Belgian? English? German? Wily den Ouden was supposed to join them to meet my mother but was detained at the last minute. A jolly evening. The two Openfelds — especially Felix — possessed that courtesy, at once stiff and lighthearted, typical of Berliners. Felix Openfeld was optimistic about the film. He already had interest from an American company. For all the years he'd been trying to persuade them to show "sports" detective comedies . . . During the dinner they took a photo, which I have here on my desk. The man with the dark, slicked-back hair, pencil mustache, and fine hands is Felix Openfeld. The two fat men slightly set back, Putmann and the wardrobe manager. The old man with the weasel head but magnificent oval eyes, Openfeld Senior. Finally, the young woman who looks like Vivien Leigh is my mother.

At the start of the film, she had a solo scene. She straightened up her room while singing and answered the phone. Felix Openfeld, who was directing, had decided to shoot in script order.

Shooting was set to begin on Friday, May 10, 1940, at Sonor Studios in Brussels. My mother was to show up at 10:30 a.m. Since she lived in Antwerp, she would take the very early train.

The day before, she received an advance on her fee, with which she bought herself a handsome leather overnight bag and some Elizabeth Arden cosmetics. She returned home at the end of the afternoon, rehearsed her role a little more, had dinner, and went to bed.

At around four in the morning, she was awoken by what she thought at first was a clap of thunder. But the noise continued—a dull, prolonged rumble. Ambulances sped by on Quai Van Dyck; people leaned out their windows. Sirens wailed all over the city. Her next-door neighbor told her in a tremulous voice that German planes were bombing the port. Then calm was restored and my mother went back to sleep. At seven o'clock, the alarm went off. In short order, she went down to wait for the streetcar on the little square, her overnight bag in hand. The streetcar never came. Groups of people walked by, murmuring to each other.

She finally found a taxi, and during the entire trip to the train station, the driver repeated like a refrain, "We're done for . . . done for . . . done for . . ."

The station concourse was crowded and my mother had a hard time pushing her way through to the platform for the Brussels train. People were swarming around the conductor, peppering him with questions: no, the train was not running. He was awaiting instructions. And the same sentence on everyone's lips: "The Germans have crossed the border . . . The Germans have crossed the border . . ."

On the 6:30 news report, the radio announcer had said the Wehrmacht had invaded Belgium, Holland, and Luxembourg.

My mother felt someone touch her arm. She turned around. Openfeld Senior, wearing a black fedora. He was unshaven, his weasel head looked half-shrunken, and his eyes were inordinately huge. Two exorbitant blue eyes in a tiny head, like the kind a pygmy might collect. He dragged her out of the station.

"We have to get to Felix in the studios . . . in Brussels . . . take a taxi . . . quickly . . . a taxi . . ."

He half-swallowed his words.

The drivers didn't want to take on such a long journey for fear of bombardments. Openfeld Senior managed to convince one with a hundred-franc bill. In the taxi, Openfeld Senior said to my mother:

"We'll split the fare."

My mother told him she had only twenty francs on her.

"No matter. We'll sort it out at the studio."

During the trip, he didn't say much. Now and then he consulted an address book and feverishly rifled through the pockets of his overcoat and jacket.

"Is that all the luggage you're taking with you?" he asked my mother, pointing to the leather overnight bag she was holding on her knees.

"All what luggage?"

"Pardon me . . . Pardon me . . . It's true, you're staying here . . ."

He murmured something inaudible. He turned to my mother.

"I never thought they wouldn't respect Belgian neutrality . . ."

He stressed the syllables of "Bel-gian neu-*tral*-i-ty." Until that day, those two words had clearly represented a vague hope, and he must have repeated them often, without really believing in them, but with so much good faith. Now they were swept aside with the rest. Belgian neutrality.

The taxi reached Brussels and they followed Avenue de Ter-vueren, where several buildings had burned to the ground. Teams of firemen were combing through the rubble. The driver asked what happened. There had been a bombardment at around eight o'clock.

In the courtyard of Sonor Studios were a van and a large convertible piled high with suitcases. When Openfeld Senior and my mother entered Soundstage B, Felix Openfeld was giving instructions to several technicians who were packing up the cameras and lights.

"We're leaving for America," Felix Openfeld told my mother in a resolute voice.

She sat on a stool. Openfeld Senior held out a cigarette case.

"Wouldn't you like to come with us? We can try to make the film over there."

"You shouldn't have any trouble at the borders," said Felix Openfeld. "You have a passport."

Their plan was to get to Lisbon as quickly as possible, via Spain. Felix Openfeld had obtained papers from the Portuguese consul—a good friend of his, he said.

"The Germans will be in Paris tomorrow and London in two weeks," Openfeld Senior declared, shaking his head.

Three of them loaded the equipment into the van: the two Openfelds and Grunebaum, a former cameraman from Tobis Film, who, although Jewish, was the spitting image of Wilhelm II. My mother knew him because, the week before, he'd wanted to do a lighting test for the close-ups. Grunebaum settled behind the wheel of the van.

"You follow me, Marc," Felix Openfeld told him.

He climbed into the convertible. My mother and Openfeld Senior squeezed into the front seat next to him. The back was taken up with several suitcases and a steamer trunk.

The studio hands wished them a safe trip. Felix Openfeld drove fast. The van kept up with them.

"We'll try to make the film in America," Openfeld Senior repeated.

My mother didn't answer. All these events were making her head spin.

At Place de Brouckère, Felix Openfeld braked in front of the Hotel Métropole. The van stopped behind him.

"Wait here . . . I'll be right back."

He ran into the hotel. A few minutes later, he returned, carrying two bottles of mineral water and a large bag.

"I bought us some sandwiches for the road."

He was about to start up when my mother suddenly got out of the car.

"I . . . have to stay . . ." she said.

They both looked at her with a vague smile. They didn't say a word to change her mind. No doubt they both figured *she* was in no danger. All things considered, she had no reason to leave. Her parents were waiting for her in Antwerp. The van left first. The two Openfelds waved good-bye. My mother waved back. Felix Openfeld peeled off, or perhaps there was a sudden gust of wind. Openfeld Senior lost his fedora, which rolled down the sidewalk. Too bad for the fedora. There wasn't a moment to lose.

My mother picked up the hat and started walking at random.

In front of the savings bank was an endless line of men and women trying to withdraw their funds. She followed Avenue du Nord to the station. There she found the same bustle, the same dazed crowd as at Antwerp station. A porter told her a train would be leaving for Antwerp at around three in the afternoon, but it might not arrive until very late at night.

At the station buffet, she sat in a corner. People came, went, left; some men were already in uniform. She heard voices around her say that general mobilization had been declared at nine o'clock. A radio in the back of the room broadcast news bulletins. The port of Antwerp had been bombed again. French troops had just crossed the border. The Germans were already in Rotterdam. Squatting near her, a woman was tying a small boy's shoelaces. Travelers bickered over a cup of coffee; others pushed and shoved; still others dragged heavy suitcases, huffing and puffing.

She had to wait until three o'clock for the train. She felt a head-ache coming on. She suddenly realized she'd lost her overnight bag, which contained the Elizabeth Arden cosmetics and the film script. Maybe she had left it at Sonor Studios, or in the car. What she still held in her hand, without noticing it until then, was Openfeld Senior's black fedora.

V

I was fifteen years old that winter, and my father and I caught the 7:15 p.m. train from the Gare de Lyon. We had spent the afternoon shopping: a raincoat and rubber overshoes for him, breeches and a riding helmet for me.

There were no other passengers in our compartment, and when the train jerked into motion, I felt a weight on my chest. Through the window, I gazed at the landscape of tracks, control towers, and idle train wagons. The cargo terminal, the customs station with its tower, and the sad little buildings of Rue Coriolis, where two silhouettes stood out in the light of a window like shadow puppets. And then we were outside of Paris.

My father, having put on his bifocals, was absorbed in a magazine. I couldn't remove my forehead from the window. The train thundered past the small suburban stations. After Maisons-Alfort, I could no longer read their names on the lit signs. The countryside began. Night had fallen, but that didn't seem to trouble my father as he continued reading his magazine, sucking on small, round green lozenges.

Rain, so slight that I hadn't noticed it at first, scratched at the black window. The light bulb in the compartment occasionally went out, but immediately came on again. The current lowered and the light enveloping us was a dusty yellow.

We should have been talking, but we didn't have much to say to each other. Now and then, my father opened his mouth and caught on the fly a lozenge that he had flicked in the air with his index finger. He stood up, pulled down his old black briefcase, and took out a folder of papers that he leafed through slowly. He underlined certain portions in pencil.

"Too bad we couldn't find a pair of boots in your size," my father said pensively, raising his eyes from the folder.

". . ."

"But Reynolde will lend you some."

". . ."

"And the breeches? You think they'll fit all right?"

"Yes, Dad."

He was never without that old black briefcase, which now lay flat on his knees, and he had no doubt brought along the folder to show Reynolde. What exactly were his relations with Reynolde? I had been present at several of their appointments, in the lobby of the Claridge. They exchanged folders or showed each other photocopied documents that they initialed, at the end of lengthy discussions. Apparently, Reynolde was devious and my father didn't trust him. Sometimes my father would go to Reynolde's home, a small private hotel on Rue Christophe-Colomb, near the Champs-Elysées. I would wait for him, walking up and down Avenue Marceau. He usually came back in a bad mood. The last time, he had clapped me on the shoulder and said mysteriously:

"Pretty soon now, Reynolde is going to find himself up the creek without a paddle. I'll see to it he makes good on his word."

Right there on the street, he had opened a folder, counted the pages one by one, verified the signatures.

My father stood up and put his black briefcase back in the luggage netting. Several minutes' stopover in Orléans. A porter walked by with a cart of sandwiches and drinks. We chose two Oranginas. The train started up again. Rain hit the window in gusts and I was afraid the glass would break. Fear settled over me little by little. The train was rushing full throttle. For how long? I forced myself to remain calm. We were sitting opposite each other, each drinking from our bottle of Orangina through a straw. Like on the beach in summer.

And I kept thinking that at that same hour, we could instead have been strolling along the boulevards and sitting at the terrace of Café Viel . . . We would have watched people go by or gone into a movie theater, instead of plunging into unknown territory in the rain. It was all my fault. Reynolde often wore what the English call a riding coat. One afternoon, I asked him whether he in fact rode. He immediately proved tireless and passionate on the subject, and I had to tell him I had some minor ability in that area, having frequented a riding academy at age eleven. Reynolde had turned to my father and proposed we spend a weekend at his estate in Sologne. They did a lot of riding there. A huge amount of riding. A good opportunity for me to get back in the saddle.

"Thank you, Monsieur Reynolde."

And my father, when we were back home, had said that Reynolde absolutely had to invite us to Sologne. There, Reynolde might agree to sign certain "important things." It was up to me to bring the conversation back around to equestrian sports as soon as possible, to convince Reynolde that I thought about nothing but horses.

It was almost nine o'clock and we had just left Ozoir-le-Vicomte. According to Reynolde's instructions, we were to get off at the next stop. My father seemed slightly nervous. He inspected his face in the mirror, combed his hair, straightened his tie, and made several arm movements to loosen his new tweed jacket: its color was of dead leaves and its shoulders overly padded. He asked me to help him on with his new raincoat. He could barely get his arms in the sleeves, so constrained was he by the tweed. With the raincoat on, he had the size and heft of a gladiator. The additional wool lining of the Burberry completely straightjacketed him, and he could scarcely lift his arm toward his black briefcase.

We waited in the corridor. The train came to a grinding halt and my father winced. We stepped down onto the platform. The rain had stopped. A single lamp, about twenty yards ahead of us, and a lit doorway at the end served as our reference points. Papa walked stiffly and awkwardly, as if encased in armor. He held his black briefcase. And I carried our two valises.

The tiny station of Breteuil-l'Etang seemed deserted. In the middle of the lobby, under the white neon light, Reynolde was waiting for us, accompanied by a young man in jodhpurs. My father shook Reynolde's hand and the latter introduced the young man. He had a name with a nobiliary particle that was linked to the building of the Suez Canal, and his first name was Jean-Gérard. I shook their hands in turn and felt a kind of queasiness in Reynolde's presence. His gray fedora, his mustache, his warm voice, and the smell of his cologne had always made me feel deeply despondent.

My father and I took our seats in the back of the Renault, while the young man sat behind the wheel and Reynolde next to him.

"Trip not too tiring?" Reynolde asked my father, in his handsome deep voice.

"No, not at all, Henri."

I was amazed that my father called him by his first name. "Jean-Gérard" started up with a jerk and my father fell back against me. I had to push him to help him back into his initial position. No two ways about it, that raincoat paralyzed him like a lead cast.

We had reached a fairly wide road and the Renault's headlights revealed trees on either side.

"We're going through Sézonnes forest," Reynolde told us with a knowing air. "Jean-Gérard" drove faster and faster.

"I'm not used to these old jalopies anymore," he said. "Real pieces of crap."

"Jean-Gé, did you tell Montaignac and Chevert about last night?" asked Reynolde.

"Not yet."

And the two of them burst out laughing. They didn't let us in on the reason for their hilarity, but rather seemed to take—or at least Reynolde did—a certain pleasure in leaving us out of their conversation.

"I can just imagine the look on Chevert's face! The stuff he believes about Monique!"

"His naïveté is touching, don't you think?"

"He's just a hick from Mauritius."

And they kept on talking about people we didn't know, with throaty guffaws. Jean-Gé sped up some more. He let go of the wheel and took a cigarette from his pocket. He lit it calmly. I shut my eyes. My father squeezed my arm. I felt like asking Reynolde if he could bring us back to the station. Right away. We'd take the first train for Paris. We had no business here. I kept silent so as not to embarrass my father or put a crimp in his plans.

"And what about your aunt?" asked Reynolde. "Is she coming Sunday?"

"You can never tell what my dear aunt will do," Jean-Gé answered.

"I adore her," Reynolde said in an affected voice. "Daisy is an admirable woman."

The Renault veered onto a small local highway.

"We're almost there," said Reynolde, turning toward my father. "This is the first time they've been to La Ménandière."

"We'll have to drink to that," said Jean-Gé, indifferently.

He braked sharply and my father, lurching forward, banged his forehead on Reynolde's neck.

"I'm so sorry, Henri," he said in a blank voice. "Please forgive me."

"You're forgiven. Did your son bring his riding outfit?"

"Yes, sir," I said.

"You can call me Henri."

"Yes, Henri Reynolde, sir."

I pulled my father out of the car. We found ourselves by a gate. Reynolde pushed it open with his shoulder. We crossed a paved courtyard framed by a house with several wings; in the middle of it I noticed a well. Light came from the front stairway.

Jean-Gé honked a dozen times, taking mischievous pleasure in blaring his horn. The door opened onto a blonde in an evening gown.

"My wife," Reynolde said to me.

"Good evening, Maggy," my father said, and I was surprised by the familiarity.

"Good evening, madam," I said, bowing.

Jean-Gé kissed her hand, bringing his lips very close but not touching the skin.

Coats were stacked haphazardly on a large sofa. She motioned for us to put down our things. I helped my father and had a hard time extracting him from his Burberry. I wondered whether we'd have to slit the sleeves open with a penknife. We entered a large room, at the back of which they had installed a table with about a dozen place settings. Several people were seated around the fireplace, among them two young women whose shoulders Jean-Gé squeezed familiarly, to their apparent delight.

Over dinner I was able to observe the guests and the surrounding décor at leisure. Reynolde had placed my father and me at the foot of the table, as if we clashed with the gathering. Jean-Gé sat between the two young ladies, one of whom spoke with an English accent. Apparently they could refuse him nothing, and he groped each of them a bit, by turns. He spoke English to the brunette, and Reynolde whispered that she was the daughter of the Duke of Northumberland. The blonde, despite her slutty demeanor, no doubt also came from an excellent family.

Maggy Reynolde presided. On either side of her was a couple that had surprised me, because both the man and the woman were wearing black velvet: sporty-cut trousers and jacket for her, very close-fitting suit for him. They looked alike, even though they were husband and wife. Same brown hair, same tan. I could tell by their rolling gait and their way of holding hands that they each took great care of themselves. They had identical, synchronized gestures, and on both of their faces floated an expression of fatuous sensuality. I learned that the man, a certain Michel Landry, was the publisher of a "sports and leisure" magazine.

Finally, next to Madame Landry was an individual of about sixty with a swarthy complexion, an emaciated face, a pencil mustache, and eyes of a very piercing blue. He wore a signet ring with a coat of arms engraved on the stone. This was the count Angèle de Chevert, and from what I gathered, he belonged to a venerable family on Mauritius, hence his skin color.

The conversation soon turned to hunting, and they talked about firearms of various origins, of which Landry detailed the respective advantages. Chevert nodded with Creole seriousness, but Jean-Gé contradicted Landry nonstop. They mentioned a duke who had a chateau nearby. Jean-Gé called him "Uncle Michel," and Reynolde simply "Michel." According to them, this duke was the top marksman of France, and this honorific, "top marksman of France," which they pronounced in tones of deep respect, made me want to retch.

My uneasiness worsened when I heard Landry ask Chevert and Reynolde:

"And how're the hounds?"

"We'll see the day after tomorrow," Chevert answered drily.

"It's going to be a superb hunt," the young blonde said in a gluttonous voice.

"You two will be the angels of the hunting party," said Jean-Gé, giving both the Englishwoman and the blonde a kiss on the neck.

"Them, too, Gé," said Reynolde, pointing to Maggy Reynolde and Landry's wife.

"Of course, of course they'll be angels."

And reaching across the table, Jean-Gé squeezed both their hands. They gave out a laugh.

Reynolde turned to me:

"Will this be your first hunt?"

"Yes, Monsieur Reynolde."

He slapped my father on the shoulder.

"Aren't you pleased, Aldo, that your boy is joining in a hunt?"

"Oh, yes, Henri, very pleased."

The others, who had ignored us until then, looked us over with curiosity.

"I'm delighted, Henri."

Papa remained impenetrable and massive behind his bifocals.

As for me, I feared I was going to pass out, which in a young man of fifteen would not have shown much fortitude.

"You couldn't have come at a better time," Landry said to me. "The best pack in France. And the greatest master of the hunt in all of Europe . . ."

"You're being too kind to Uncle Michel," said Jean-Gé, smugly.

"No, Jean-Gérard, he is not being kind," Chevert said gravely. "There have been only three great huntsmen in the past hundred years: Anne d'Uzès, Philippe de Vibraye, and your uncle . . ."

That pronouncement was followed by a moment of silence. Everyone was moved, Reynolde first and foremost. Chevert sat very stiffly, chin raised, as if he had just proffered a statement for the ages. My father tried to suppress a small nervous cough. It was Jean-Gérard who broke the spell.

"You really know quite a lot out there on Mauritius!" he said, addressing Chevert.

"Please don't mention it," said Chevert, curtly. Then he added: "Yes, we do know quite a lot on Mauritius."

They brought in an imposing platter. A woman with her hair in a bun set it on the table, and Landry's wife, the young Englishwoman, and the blonde clapped their hands.

"Marvelous," Landry exclaimed.

"An authentic Chaumont peacock," said Reynolde.

And he jerked his thumb in a brutal gesture that clashed with the distinguished conversation I'd just been hearing.

"They say it's an aphrodisiac," said Landry's wife. "Did you know that, Maggy?"

The woman offered the platter to my father and me so that we could serve ourselves.

"Let me explain," Reynolde said to us, articulating his words as if he were speaking to the deaf. "A Chaumont peacock is fed on cedar buds and stuffed with truffles and nuts."

I held myself perfectly still to keep from gagging.

"Try it! You'll tell me what you think!"

After a while, he noticed that I hadn't touched my dinner.

"Go on, try it! It would be criminal to leave that in your plate, my boy!"

At that instant, a kind of metamorphosis occurred in me. They were all—except for Papa—giving me cold, dismayed looks.

"Go on, boy! Have a taste!" Reynolde repeated.

My pathological timidity and docility had vanished and I suddenly understood how superficial they all were. I felt as if I had shed a dead skin. I retorted in an implacable voice:

"No, sir, I will not eat one bite of this."

My father turned to me, mouth agape. The others, too, whose dinners I had surely ruined. All at once, it occurred to me that I could do them much more harm than they could ever do me, and immediately a wave of compassion and remorse washed over me.

"Forgive me," I stammered. "Forgive me."

It was only after the liqueurs had been served that the atmosphere relaxed again. Naturally, they still gave me surreptitious glances, and to reassure them I forced myself to smile. Taking a deep breath, I even declared to Reynolde:

"I am very happy and thrilled to be able to join the hunt on Sunday, Monsieur Reynolde."

I think they ended up forgetting the incident. The heavy burgundies from dinner helped. They continued their libations. Pear brandy, plum brandy, cognac—they sampled them all. The women, too, drank heavily, especially the Englishwoman and Maggy Reynolde. Our glasses, Papa's and mine, remained full, for we hadn't dared refuse when we were offered. And the conversation still revolved around hunting.

According to Chevert, one feature distinguished "Uncle Michel" from every other master of the hunt in France: he had reinstituted the "torchlight quarry."

"A magnificent spectacle, Aldo!" cried Reynolde.

My father, in his soft voice, asked what they meant by a "torchlight quarry." Jean-Gé, who had drunk more than anyone, gave a sad smile.

"Because the gentleman doesn't know what a torchlight quarry is?"

Chevert explained that on such occasions, the entire staff, in baize breeches and traditional French costumes, carried torches while the hunting party . . . I was barely listening. His voice was lost amid the laughs and exclamations of Jean-Gé and his two girlfriends. Maggy Reynolde and Landry's wife chatted between themselves, and Landry caressed his wife's cheek with the tip of his thumb, while talking to Reynolde. Jean-Gé, for his part, was resting his hand on the Englishwoman's shoulder, but neither she nor the blonde seemed to mind. And Chevert, in an almost inaudible voice, continued his disquisition.

What were we waiting for, my father and I? Shouldn't he have taken advantage of the general relaxation to pull Reynolde into a corner and get him to sign his "papers"? After that, we would have slipped away. But he simply smoked a cigarette. Nothing disturbed his impassiveness. He was deeply sunken into the armchair and not budging. Anyway, he knew how to go about it better than I did.

Reynolde stoked the fire. The bricks of the immense hearth had a slightly garish tint. Thick, light-colored paneling covered the walls. On the coffee table sat a horseshoe-shaped paperweight and a photo book about the Spanische Reitschule in Vienna. I noticed other accessories displayed on the wall, to the left of the fireplace. Stirrups, bits, and whips of every variety. English etchings of hunting scenes and a small, carriage-shaped drinks cart completed the equestrian décor.

I was having a hard time keeping my eyes open. I heard a murmur of conversation and Papa saying from time to time, "Yes, of course, Henri . . . Naturally, Henri . . ." The Englishwoman let out shrill laughs. Chevert finally stood up:

"Well, I'll bid you all good night."

He kissed the ladies' hands with some emphasis. Jean-Gé and his two girlfriends took their leave soon after. Reynolde told them to take the large bedroom on the third floor if they wanted to spend the night here and if they thought the bed was large enough for three. The Landrys withdrew, shooting each other suggestive glances. Moreover, all evening long, Landry had not stopped caressing his wife's legs.

"Aldo, you don't mind sleeping in the ground-floor bedroom with your son, do you?" Reynolde asked my father.

"Not in the slightest, Henri."

A room with a low ceiling and whitewashed walls. No furniture, save two rustic-style twin beds and two nightstands. I set our bags down.

Reynolde left us for a moment to go find a second bedside lamp.

"You should go kiss Madame Reynolde good night," my father said to me.

I left the bedroom and headed toward the large room where we had dined. Maggy Reynolde was there alone, by the fire. She looked surprised to see me. I kissed her on the cheek. Immediately, her two hands gripped the back of my neck and her lips pressed against mine. At fifteen, I had never kissed a woman her age. Her hand slid down to my belt, which she tried to undo. I slipped and we tumbled onto one of the plaid armchairs. Sounds of voices in the hallway. She struggled, but I could no longer break away from her. My forehead glued to her chest, I let myself be overcome, even while in an embrace, by a curious somnolence. She had that comfortable blondness of certain members of the Comédie-Française, whom I would watch perform in Sunday matinees.

When we stood up, she pulled me out of the room. Reynolde and my father were at the door of our bedroom. My father was showing Reynolde a typed sheet. The latter was holding a pen.

"Here," Reynolde said to me, "I brought you this. You'll have to study it all night for me."

He handed me a small volume on whose cover I read the words *Sport Hunting*.

"Good night," my father said to him.

"Good night, Aldo. And thank you for your advice. You can count on us. And you"—he pointed at me—"I'll bring you up to the stables tomorrow morning for some practice."

"Good night," Maggy Reynolde said to us. She was yawning.

We stretched out on our twin beds and my father turned off his bedside lamp.

"This time," he said to me, indicating the typed sheet, "he's all but 'up the creek.' Just a little more patience, old man. They really are a formidable bunch."

He snorted with laughter, and since it was contagious, we both buried our heads in our pillows so as not to be heard.

Papa fell asleep very quickly. I opened the book and spent part of the night learning about the *horrifying* sport they called hunting.

The next morning, Reynolde woke us at around eight. He was wearing riding breeches and asked me to put on mine. My father thought it wise to slip on his rubber overshoes.

After having what Reynolde called by the English word "breakfast," we went out via the French doors and crossed through a well-manicured garden whose limits were marked by a white fence. Behind it was a large field, a stable with three stalls, and a circular bridle path. The horse was already saddled and harnessed. All I had to do was climb on.

Reynolde had positioned himself in the middle of the riding hall and my father a good distance from the track. He was afraid. I was too, but I was trying to keep calm in front of Reynolde. He was holding a whip. He cracked it like a circus trainer and the horse took off at a trot.

"Lift your ass, boy!"

Now he'd taken on the voice of an army officer. He pointed his chin and cracked his whip again. For no reason. For the fun of it.

"Rising trot! Knees closer in!"

He came up to me and tapped gently on my left calf and heel.

"These must not move! Squeeze in. Heels lower!"

He went back to the middle of the riding hall.

"Don't get caught in the stirrups! Heels lower!"

And he cracked his whip. Three times in a row.

My father didn't dare look at me. He lowered his head.

"You're a bit rusty," shouted Reynolde, "but you'll get the hang of it again pretty fast. Now, sitting trot!"

And again the whip. After each crack, he saluted an invisible audience with a slight nod of his head.

"You can come closer, Aldo."

"No, thanks, Henri," my father answered in a hesitant voice.

"The knees! For the love of God! Didn't you hear me? Gallop!"

He was turning nasty. He lashed out his whip as if to splatter a fly in midair and it made a sound like a firecracker.

It lasted a good two hours. You're on a horse and you turn in circles without knowing why. And the horse doesn't know why, either. In the middle of the track, some guy you hardly know is giving you orders, brandishing a whip. And your father is several yards away, worried and silent and staring at the tips of his rubber overshoes.

"That'll be good enough for tomorrow," Reynolde said to me, patting me on the shoulder.

There were four of us around the lunch table. Reynolde, Angèle de Chevert, my father, and me. Jean-Gé had taken the Landrys and Maggy Reynolde to "his uncle's chateau," several miles away.

"They might have told us," Reynolde commented.

During lunch, my father took from the inner pocket of his jacket a sheet of paper that he showed Chevert.

"You can sign, Angèle," Reynolde said. But already my father was handing Chevert the huge fountain pen that we had bought together in Passage du Lido.

"Sign it, Angèle. Aldo will see that we're not just playing around."

Chevert did as told. My father blew on the ink to dry it, then carefully folded the sheet and put it back in his pocket.

He, normally so impervious, must have been feeling a keen elation, since I read on his lips these words that no one heard:

"Up the creek."

"That's one thing out of the way," Reynolde stated. "And now, let's go see the hounds."

Reynolde drove the Renault. We followed a narrow road and, after about ten minutes, we stopped in front of an Anglo-Norman–style chalet. The dogs were in a fenced enclosure. Little by little, their barking took on a worrisome intensity that jangled my nerves. They threw themselves against the wire fencing and my father jumped back.

"Don't be scared, Aldo," Reynolde said to him in a protective tone.

Chevert shrugged. He spoke to the dogs with a vulgarity that shocked me. A man was approaching with great strides, wearing a dark blue uniform like a stationmaster. He doffed his cap, held it with both hands against his chest, and, without even a glance at Reynolde, nodded to Chevert.

"Good afternoon, Your Excellency."

"Is the pack in top form?"

"Yes, Your Excellency."

"Sparks are really going to fly tomorrow," said Chevert, rubbing his hands together.

"And how, Your Excellency!" His lips opened onto a toothless mouth.

"His Grace the duke will be in seventh heaven!" said Reynolde, pitifully soliciting a glance from the man.

But the latter didn't pay him the slightest attention. He shook hands with Chevert and headed off.

"The keeper of the hounds," Reynolde solemnly informed me.

My father and I remained in front of the wire fencing, contemplating the dogs that jumped and barked more and more frenetically. They would gladly have torn us to shreds, but it wasn't their fault and I forgave them. Nearly all of them had large pug noses, wide, frank eyes, and white patches on their fur.

We returned to La Ménandière. Reynolde and Chevert wanted to take a nap, and Papa and I remained in the salon. It was there that he announced he was taking the four o'clock train back to Paris. He seemed amazed when I said I wanted to go with him.

"But, Reynolde is counting on you taking part in the hunt," he answered in a feeble voice.

He was afraid Reynolde would be surprised and offended by my departure and suddenly grow suspicious. He told me he had obtained "all the signatures," but Reynolde had to be handled with care for a while longer, or things could still go "pear-shaped." I repeated my desire to return to Paris right away. I refused to stay in this backwater one more day.

He promised to talk to Reynolde and, if need be, invent an excuse that would justify my sudden departure.

Reynolde came toward us. My father told him I had to be in Paris that very evening to welcome a Venezuelan uncle.

"Think carefully about this," Reynolde said to me with a certain severity. "You're going to miss something unique."

My father made a second attempt, but so timidly that he didn't even finish his sentence.

And so I turned to Reynolde and said in a whisper:

"I'll stay."

"You've made the right choice," Reynolde said. "It's going to be a magnificent hunt." And he looked at me gratefully.

We drove my father to the train. Reynolde was at the wheel of the Renault, Chevert next to him, Papa and I in back. As on the way in, Papa had put on his constricting raincoat. His face reflected a sharp satisfaction, and I could see that he was suppressing a recurrent desire to laugh.

On the platform, we didn't exchange a word. Chevert and Reynolde were too nearby.

"I'm counting on you, Aldo," Reynolde said to my father. "We're giving you carte blanche. Keep Chevert and me posted. And I promise, you can have faith in us. Don't listen to spiteful gossips."

"Yes, of course, Henri," my father answered affably.

As he climbed aboard, he just had time to whisper in my ear:

"This time, they are totally 'up the creek.'"

The train jerked forward. He waved for my benefit. There was nothing more he could do for me, despite his great kindness.

On the way back, we took a different route from the one leading to La Ménandière. We soon drove through a gateway and followed a gently sloping gravel path.

"You have to see the duke's chateau," Reynolde said to me, "and be introduced to Michel. Tomorrow, he'll be your master of the hunt."

The chateau was in half-Renaissance, half-medieval style, with crenels, turrets, pilasters with arabesques, and large sculpted dormers. A park surrounded it.

One floor up, we entered a large room, dark and paneled. There, on the sofas, I recognized the Landrys and Jean-Gé with his two girl-friends. A few logs had just finished turning to ash in the back of the fireplace.

"Uncle Michel hasn't shown up yet," Jean-Gé said in a slurred voice.

Later, Reynolde and Chevert left me alone with the others. Night was falling and, as they didn't put on the lights, we were all shrouded in semidarkness. I think Landry took advantage to caress his wife, whose raised skirt uncovered her thighs. As for Jean-Gé, he was still lazily fondling the Englishwoman and the blonde. And I wondered what I was doing there, in the lair of the "top marksman of France," but a leaden torpor held me in my chair.

Time passed. Reynolde, his wife, and Chevert returned. They had switched on the lamps. I understood that they were waiting for the duke's return to have dinner. After a half-hour, he made his entrance: a man of medium height who held himself very erect. He had the head of a bull terrier, a nose too short and turned up, large, pale eyes, and jowls. Skin like a shark, wavy hair, and a booming voice. Reynolde introduced us. He barely acknowledged me.

I would have liked to see the duchess, but she was out that evening. An angular brunette replaced her, with the watchful eyes of a former starlet. The duke took her hand now and again. Her name was Monique.

Talk during the meal was again of hunting. And of the next day's torchlight quarry, for which the duke had just selected the site. Reynolde had affected Jean-Gé's dental accent and called the duke — but was he really a duke? — "Dear old Michel." Jean-Gé called him "Uncle Michel," in a sarcastically respectful tone.

From their conversation, I understood that the duke was a conscientious and disciplined man who belonged to the Jockey Club, the Automobile Club, and the Tastevins de Bourgogne.

They completely ignored my presence, which was fine with me. They even forgot to serve me the venison patés, meats in sauce, and heavy wines that my fragile system couldn't have handled.

We took our leave at around ten and the duke, in bawdy, jocular tones, advised against "making whoopee" that night, as we had to be in top form for the hunt. The brunette followed him.

I didn't sleep a wink all night and the next morning I was already up when Reynolde came into my room. He was again wearing the red jacket with gold braiding of the duke's hunting party, and looked like the tamer from the Médrano Circus whom I'd admired when I was a child. They all downed a copious breakfast, and I had a glass of mineral water. Chevert wore the same uniform as Reynolde, and so did the Landrys. I stood out from the rest of them. On Maggy's and Mme Landry's faces, I read great excitement.

"Feeling tip-top, darling?" Landry asked gently. And he stroked his wife's hand.

"Oh, yes! I can't wait to see this!"

"Neither can I," sighed Maggy Reynolde.

Chevert whistled. Reynolde stood up.

"Time to go get the 'report,'" he said.

"It's at the Beringhem crossing, near the lodge," Chevert said.

We piled into the Renault. Reynolde drove. Five horses were waiting in front of the hunting lodge, their bridles held by stable boys.

"You take Rex," Reynolde snapped at me, nodding at a large bay.

We were early. We went inside the lodge, which was shaped like a pagoda. On the wall was a stuffed boar's head, smiling with its human lips. They had built a fire.

A rifle was hanging above the mantel. Reynolde took it down and started to show me how to use it. He loaded it. For the first time in my life, someone was giving me a shooting lesson, and I listened intently. One after the other, the members of the party poured in, sporting the red-and-gold outfit.

"Mount up, old man!" Reynolde said to me.

Outside, Chevert was kissing the hand of a heavily surrounded woman with gray hair and the mannish face of a dowager. On their horses, Jean-Gé, the Englishwoman, and the blonde called laughingly to each other. Landry held out the stirrup to his wife. Reynolde and Maggy sidled toward the duke, who was astride a huge white horse, making it rear. And all around, the red-and-gold outfits fluttered. Finally, a bloodhound keeper, bareheaded, announced that the stag was at Estoile, a very small birch wood, nearby to the right.

I picked up the rifle and stole outside. I ran for half a mile, up to the little birch wood, perhaps the one the bloodhound keeper had announced to the members of the party. I flattened on my stomach, in the odor of wet earth and dead leaves.

I thought of my father repeating his little sentence: "They'll all be up the creek." Yes, he'd proved to be exceedingly useless and touchingly oblivious. Things were much more serious and tragic than he realized. Sure enough, Reynolde's little book had taught me exactly how the operation unfolded. It all kicked off with the opening fanfare. What would the hounds do? I had to keep from shaking. And most of all, try to aim true. Not fire on the women. Have the good fortune, with my first round, to blow Reynolde's head to pieces, or the duke's. Or Landry's. Or Jean-Gé's. Then all the others would arrive with their dogs and their attendants, and though we were in Sologne, in the French heartland, it would be just like Warsaw.

VI

It was an evening in early October in the year 1973. A Saturday, seven o'clock. In the bookstore on Rue de Marivaux where I happened to be, they had turned on the radio. The music was suddenly interrupted, and they announced that war had begun, in the Middle East, against the Jews.

I left the bookstore, with several old volumes of Porto-Riche's theater under my arm. I walked quickly, at random. Still, I remember that I walked by the Madeleine church and that I followed Boulevard Haussmann.

That evening, I sensed that something was coming to an end. My youth? I was certain nothing would ever be the same, and I can pinpoint the exact moment when everything changed for me: as I left the bookstore. But no doubt many people, at the same hour, were experiencing the same anxiety, because it was that evening that what they call the "crisis" began, and we entered a new era.

It was dark. On Place Saint-Augustin, on the balcony of a building, letters were shining: JEANNE GATINEAU. The square was abuzz with activity and I walked by the display window of a shop where I used to try on shoes and winter parkas when I was a child. I found myself at the beginning of Avenue de Messine and followed it without meeting a soul. I heard the shuddering of the plane trees. Up ahead, at the end of the avenue, facing the gilded gates of Parc Monceau, stood a café whose name I've forgotten. I sat at a table, near the windows of the glassed-in terrace, and before me I saw Rue de Lisbonne, its rectilinear façades vanishing toward the horizon. I ordered an espresso. I thought about the war, and my eyes followed the slow fall of a dead leaf, a leaf from the plane tree opposite me.

There were only two of us in the place at that late hour. They had shut off the fluorescents in the main room, but an overly bright light still fell on the terrace.

He was sitting near me, two or three tables away, and staring at a building façade on the other side of the avenue. A man of about sixty, whose navy-blue overcoat was of a heavy and outdated cut. I remember his face, a bit unfocused, round, pale eyes, and his gray mustache and hair, which was meticulously combed back. He held a cigarette between his lips, on which he puffed distractedly. On the table, a glass half-full of some pink liquid. I don't believe he noticed my presence. Still, at a certain point, he turned his head toward me, and I still wonder whether I did or didn't make eye contact. Did he see me? He sipped his pink drink. He continued his observation of the building façade, perhaps waiting for someone to come outside. He rummaged in a plastic bag leaning against his chair and took out a small package shaped like a pyramid, sky blue in color.

I got up and went downstairs to the telephone. I verified in the 1973 phone book the address of someone I was supposed to meet the next day, then looked up other names at random. Some of them, which evoked a distant past, were now listed again, and I went from surprise to surprise: CATONI DE WIET, unreachable for fifteen years, reappeared at 80 Avenue Victor-Hugo—Passy 47-22. On the other hand, no trace left of "Reynolde," or of "Douglas Eyben," or of "Toddie Werner," or of "Georges Dismaïlov," or of so many others that we'll run into again someday . . . I sometimes amuse myself with these pointless verifications. It lasted fifteen or twenty minutes, more or less.

When I came back to the terrace, the man with the navy-blue overcoat was bent forward with his chest and head on the table. I could see the top of his skull. His right arm was hanging limp; the other one was folded and seemed to be protecting the glass of grenadine and the plastic bag, like a schoolboy who doesn't want his classmate to crib his answers. He wasn't moving. I paid for my espresso. The waiter tapped him gently on the shoulder, then shook him a bit more forcefully, without getting any reaction. After a while, it became clear he was dead. They called the police. I was standing near his table in a daze, staring at him. His glass was empty and the plastic bag sat open. What was in it? The waiter and someone who must have been the owner—a fat redhead in an open-necked white shirt—kept asking each other, in voices that grew increasingly shrill and staccato, how something like this could have happened.

The police van stopped near Rue de Monceau. Two uniforms and a plainclothesman joined us. I turned away. I think they were making sure the man was dead.

The plainclothes detective asked me to follow him as a "witness," and I didn't dare tell him I hadn't seen a thing. The café owner was sweating and fixed me with a worried stare. He probably thought I was going to refuse, because when I said yes he let out a sigh and nodded in gratitude. He told them, "This gentleman will explain everything," and he couldn't wait for us to leave. They carried the man out on a stretcher to the police van. I followed, holding his plastic bag.

The van turned onto Rue de Lisbonne. It went faster and faster down that empty street and I had to grip the edge of the bench to keep from falling. The plainclothesman was on the opposite bench. A blond with a face like a sheep and marcelled hair. The stretcher was between us. I took care not to look at the man. The blond with the sheep's face offered me a cigarette that I refused. My left hand was still clutching the plastic bag.

At the police station, they asked me what had happened and typed up my deposition. No big deal. I explained that the man had collapsed on the table soon after drinking his grenadine. They rummaged in the black plastic bag, from which they pulled a professional-grade compact tape recorder and the sky-blue pyramid-shaped package that I'd already noticed. It contained a pastry of the type called a napoleon.

In one of his jacket pockets, they found a leather wallet containing his identity card, an old photograph, and various other papers. And so we learned that his name was André Bourlagoff, born in Saint Petersburg in 1913. He had been a French citizen since 1934 and worked for a company on Rue de Berri that rented out tape recorders. His job consisted of retrieving the tape recorders at the homes of customers who hadn't returned them on time. For this, he received a rather paltry salary. He lived in a furnished apartment on Rue de la Convention, in the 15th arrondissement.

The photograph was very dog-eared and at least fifty years old, judging by the clothes and décor. It showed two privileged-looking young people sitting on a sofa, and between them a curly-haired child of about two.

One file card concerned the tape recorder that Bourlagoff was carrying in his plastic bag. It gave the address of the customer who had rented the machine — 45 Rue de Courcelles — with his name and the fee he had paid. Bourlagoff, when he'd sat at the café terrace, had therefore just come from 45 Rue de Courcelles, a bit farther down the street.

They gave me this information as a courtesy. I had asked because I wanted to know the name of that man and, if possible, a few more details.

I left the police station. It was ten in the evening. Again I walked across Place Saint-Augustin and the name JEANNE GATINEAU still shone on the balcony, its glare softened by the fog. Farther on, the sound of my footsteps echoed beneath the deserted arcades of Rue de Rivoli. I stopped at the edge of Place de la Concorde. This fog worried me. It enveloped everything — the streetlamps, the lit fountains, the obelisk, the statues representing French cities — in a blanket of silence. And it smelled of ether.

I thought about the war that had started up again that day, in the East, and also about André Bourlagoff. Had the customer greeted him politely, earlier, when he had come to take back the tape recorder and ask for his money?

His was a thankless and rather obscure job. What path had he followed, this André Bourlagoff, from his furnished room on Rue de la Convention to 45 Rue de Courcelles? Had he gone on foot? In that case, he had surely crossed the Seine via the Bir-Hakeim bridge, with the rattle of the elevated trains overhead.

His life had begun in Russia, in Saint Petersburg, in the year 1913. One of those ochre palaces on the river. I traveled back in time to that year and slipped through the half-open door into the large sky-blue nursery. You were asleep, your tiny hand sticking out of the crib. Seems that today, you went for a long stroll up to the gardens of the Tauride and had a good appetite at dinner. Mlle. Coudreuse told me so. This evening, we'll stay at home, your mother and I, in the company of a few friends. Winter is coming and no doubt we'll go spend a few days with you in the Crimea, or in our villa in Nice . . . But what good is it to make plans and think about the future? This evening, the clock in the hallway still rings the hours in crystalline tones. It watches over your childish slumber and protects you, like the lights, blinking, over there, near the Islands.

VII

Yes, of course, in that little cinema in the Ternes neighborhood, the bonus feature they were showing was *Captain Van Mers.*

Paris, a Saturday evening in August. After the main feature, most of the viewers had left the theater and only about a dozen people remained. When the lights dimmed, I felt a knot in my stomach.

The credits rolled by using a time-honored device: the pages of a diary turning slowly to the sound of gentle music. The letters were brownish and elongated. Bella's name came before Bruce Tellegen's, even though they both had lead roles. My own name came after that of the cameraman, with the heading "screenplay and dialogues by." Finally, on the last page, red gothic lettering blared out: CAPTAIN VAN MERS.

A sizable yacht heads for an island that is still just a tiny green smudge on the horizon. And we see Bella standing on the prow, hair floating in the wind. The emerald of the sea and the blue of the sky are a bit too vibrant and bleed into each other. We had huge problems with the color. Nor was the sound quality entirely right. Nor the acting, for that matter. And the plot wasn't especially compelling. But that evening, in that nearly empty auditorium, watching the projection of *Captain Van Mers* . . .

Seven years earlier, a producer named Yvon Stocklin had called me very late one evening, setting an appointment for the next day at his place. We would talk about a "project." I didn't know this Stocklin and I've often wondered how he had learned of my existence.

He welcomed me into an apartment on Avenue d'Iéna that contained not a stick of furniture. I followed him through the parade of empty rooms and we arrived at a salon with two folding chairs. We sat facing each other. He took a pipe from his pocket, stuffed it conscientiously, lit it, drew a puff, and held it between his teeth. I couldn't look away from that pipe, which was the only stable and reassuring object in the midst of the emptiness and desolation of those surroundings. Later, I learned that Yvon Stocklin spent entire nights sitting on his bed and smoking his pipe. It was his way of fighting the unstable, fanciful nature of his job as a producer. An entire life frittered away for nada . . . When he smoked his pipe, he could finally feel like a man of substance, a "rock" — felt like he could, in his words, "put the pieces together."

That evening, he immediately launched into his "idea."

He wanted to hire me to adapt a novel for the screen, and rather than call one of those "top of the line" professional screenwriters with whom he had often worked — he cited two or three names that, since then, have been forgotten — he preferred to give carte blanche to a "youngster," and a "writer," to boot. It was a "fabulous" book, to which he'd just acquired the rights. It was called *Capitaine des Mers du Sud:* Captain of the South Seas. But because of the mainly Anglo-Dutch co-producers, they changed the film's title to *Captain Van Mers.* Would I accept the "package"? With him, you had to decide very fast and "sight unseen." No one ever regretted it. Yes or no?

Well, then, yes.

In that case, Georges Rollner, the director, was expecting us for dinner at the Pré Catelan.

The orchestra was playing waltzes and Rollner talked effusively. He repeated to Stocklin that it was a good idea to hire a "kid" like me. Both of them must have been at least in their fifties. Later, I found out that Stocklin had started out at Pathé-Natan. Rollner's name wasn't unfamiliar to me. He had had some hits in the '50s, notably a poignant story about surgeons. He had gradually drifted into directing after having worked as studio manager, production assistant, and production manager. As much as Stocklin's brachycephalic face, ruddy complexion, and blue eyes gave an illusory impression of solidity (he claimed to be of Savoyard stock), Rollner's black eyes, outline, and smile gave off a fragile charm. Toward the end of the meal, I nonetheless asked about the novel.

Rollner immediately pulled from his jacket pocket a book of minuscule proportions and handed it to me. The novel was dated 1907 and had been published by Edouard Guillaume for his popular collection "Lotus Alba."

"I'm entrusting you with *Captain of the South Seas*," he said, smiling. "I hope we'll do some good work together."

The next day, I signed my contract at Stocklin's, in Rollner's presence. I immediately received six hundred thousand old francs, my name would figure on the poster and display advertising, and I would get a 2 percent share of "profits net of Production costs." Stocklin decided I should leave the next day with Rollner for Port-Cros, where the movie was to be filmed. There, we'd work on the screenplay, which had to be "sewn up" as quickly as possible. Shooting would begin the following month. The crew was already standing by. They hadn't yet cast all the parts, but that would take only a few more days.

In Port-Cros, Rollner and I settled into a small hotel at the back of a bay. He suggested I work on my own for a week. He left me "complete latitude" and recommended that I go straight into writing a "continuity."

The book was so tiny and the type so microscopic that I had to face the facts: I would never manage to read *Captain of the South Seas* without a magnifying glass. The hotel didn't have a magnifying glass. We rented a motorboat and went to Giens. We didn't find one there, either. This seemed to amuse Rollner. He saw no reason not to continue our quest all the way to Toulon, but fortunately an optician in Hyères provided me with a loupe.

I got up late and worked afternoons. The story was about nineteenth-century pirates, but Rollner wanted it set in the present.

For relaxation, I would join him in a little inlet he'd discovered. He dove continually from a pyramid-shaped boulder. He even executed a graceful swan dive. Diving had always had great importance and therapeutic value for him. It was the best way, he explained, to "recharge your batteries."

I ended up thinking we were on holiday, he and I, like two old friends. The weather was glorious, and since it was June there weren't any tourists yet. We dined on the hotel terrace, facing the bay. Rollner told me about his time in the RAF during the war, the most important event of his life. He had enlisted because he wanted to prove to himself and everyone else "that one could be Jewish and still be a flying ace." Which he had been.

In two weeks, I finished the "adaptation" of *Captain of the South Seas.* I admit I dashed off the last thirty pages. When Rollner asked me to read him what I'd written, I felt a keen apprehension. Having never done this type of work, I was especially afraid that my "shot breakdown" wouldn't be to his liking. (In fact, I'd scrupulously followed the order of the book, paragraph by paragraph.) As I read, Rollner's attention began to flag; his mind was elsewhere. When I finished, he congratulated me. "Very lively, nice goddamn work," he said in an affectionate voice. Then, after a moment's reflection:

"Do you think you could add a sentence to the dialogue, somewhere?"

"Yes, sure, of course," I said eagerly.

"Here it is . . . At a certain moment, the guy will say, 'Just bear in mind, mister, that one can be Jewish and still be a flying ace . . .'"

Even though that remark had nothing to do with the story line, I managed to get it into the hero's mouth.

Rollner was dead set on it. In fact, it was the only thing that mattered to him, as the prospect of making this movie visibly plunged him into a state of profound lethargy.

The crew—a rather minimal one—arrived one Sunday evening, carrying all the equipment. The yacht on which we'd shoot the first scenes was sitting in port; the producers had rented it from a Belgian baron. The supporting cast (three women and two men) disembarked on the island the following Tuesday.

We waited for the two stars, Bella F. and Bruce Tellegen.

In the middle of the afternoon, a huge motor craft stopped at the pontoon dock of the hotel. Two men got out, bearing a stretcher, while a third hoisted numerous valises of tawny-colored leather onto the quay. Rollner and I were sitting on the hotel terrace, and I think the cameraman and script girl were also with us. The others came forward. We immediately recognized the person they were carrying on the stretcher: Bruce Tellegen. Rollner stood up and waved. Tellegen had a three-day beard and his face was bathed in sweat. He was shivering with fever. When he saw Rollner, he said in a moribund voice:

"Georges Rollner, I presume?"

But already the two attendants were hauling him to his room. He remained bedridden. Rollner told me Tellegen was suffering the residual effects of an old case of malaria, and that this threatened to compromise the film. But he liked him and wanted to keep him, and personally he, Rollner, couldn't care less if those insurance "bastards" now refused to "cover" Tellegen.

Meanwhile, Bella F. had arrived as well.

The first scenes took place on board the yacht, and since Tellegen didn't figure in them, Rollner began shooting. He worked rather sluggishly, and I suspected he was hoping Tellegen's illness would drag on long enough to give him an excuse to stop filming.

He asked me to stay in Port-Cros during shooting, as we might have to modify the screenplay, but to the end it remained exactly as I'd written it.

Twenty years earlier, Bruce Tellegen, our lead, had been one of Hollywood's most visible young actors. He excelled in adventure films and swashbucklers, playing Lagardère, Quentin Durward, and the Scarlet Pimpernel with such vivacity and charm that he immediately earned great popularity. Then he took on different roles: missionary, explorer, solitary navigator. Each time, he played a hero of irreproachable purity whom life had sullied and who had been driven to despair by the cruelty of his fellow men. Audiences were moved by this mysterious, angelic figure who struggled against evil, often in vain and even with a certain masochism, since these films inevitably contained a scene in which Tellegen was savagely tortured . . . They said he liked those scenes. With each film, he lost a little of his magnetism. Drinking had a lot to do with it. So did age, for as he approached forty, he could no longer play roles that demanded exceptional physical fitness. And then, one morning, he had awoken with white hair.

Bella—I'll call her by her first name—was about fifteen years older than I and already had a long career behind her. At seventeen, she had been the very model of those starlets who vamped for paparazzi at the Cannes Film Festival. After that, she had a few successes. As she was a good dancer and could speak fluent English, they hired her to play supporting roles in American musical comedies. Back in France, in the early fifties, bathing in the glamour of her Hollywood sojourn, she starred in several films directed by competent journeymen. The public liked her well enough. But that was a decade ago.

She was a tiny brunette with green eyes, prominent cheekbones, a turned-up nose, and an obdurate forehead.

Tellegen was back on his feet after a week, but he had lost twenty pounds and walked unsteadily, often using a cane. Rollner shot the outdoor scenes with him first.

I saw very little of the actual filming, as I got up too late. Rollner was famous for his slow pace and his meticulousness. He had a hard time choosing which angle he wanted, and it caused him acute anxiety. The sound engineer, who had worked with him before, told me the editing caused him even more torment: on those occasions, he had seen Rollner on the verge of suicide, and he didn't use the word lightly. Still, after a few days, *Captain Van Mers* had an unusual effect on Rollner. He appeared to doze off between takes. One time, he fell fast asleep.

It's true that the story line was not terribly original. Bella, on the prow, is transfixed by the island where she and her five friends, rich idle youth on a cruise, are about to land. They have no moral compass, and "an atmosphere of depravity" reigns aboard the yacht. On the island, they meet the "Captain of the South Seas," a retired merchant seaman who has lived there for the past twenty years. A pure soul, to whom Tellegen lent the face of a former young lead. Bella falls in love with him, despite the age difference, and abandons her friends to go live with the "Captain" in the solitude of this lush island.

Tellegen and Bella made an odd couple, he so tall, she so slight that you would have taken them for father and small daughter. I remember one afternoon when I watched a scene being filmed. Bella and Tellegen take their first walk in the heart of the island. The Captain of the South Seas declares to her:

"With you, I feel like I've become young again . . ."

To which she replies:

"Why did you say that? You *are* young . . ."

It was very hot and Tellegen's shirt was drenched with sweat. He changed it every ten minutes. He collapsed onto his folding chair and they retouched his makeup. Bella couldn't stand the sun either. She was in a bad mood. Rollner, in his eternal navy-blue anorak, tried to joke with them and gave them stage directions. During pauses, Tellegen loosened his leather corset. He put it on when the scene required him to remain on his feet for long periods. It was hard for him to stand straight.

We returned to the hotel at dusk. We had to walk for about a quarter of an hour and the crew went on ahead. Bella, Rollner, Tellegen, and I remained alone. Before starting out, Tellegen offered each of us the bottle of vodka that he was never without and urged us to take a good swig. It would buck us up.

Rollner led the way, supporting Tellegen. The latter rested the palm of his hand on Georges's right shoulder and leaned on his cane. Bella and I followed a few yards behind. She had taken my arm. The moonlight was lovely and the path sometimes disappeared beneath the heather, making it hard to follow. The air was thick with the scent of pine and eucalyptus, and still today that smell brings back our nocturnal trek. The sound of our footsteps disturbed a silence that grew deeper and deeper, and Bella rested her head on my shoulder. After a while, Tellegen showed signs of fatigue.

He limped, stumbled, and caught himself in extremis on Georges Rollner's arm. He stopped short. He stood there, face bathed in sweat, eyes vacant, and signaled for us to keep going. In the moonlight, he seemed to have aged another ten years.

Rollner and I finally managed to drag him to the hotel. His teeth were chattering. This was the same man I had seen, when I was a child, agile and slim in *The Scarlet Pimpernel.*

The four of us met up at the same table in the hotel dining room. Bella had already made a film with Rollner and they reminisced together.

After dinner, Bella, Rollner, the sound engineer, and the cameraman engaged in a few hands of poker. I remained behind with Tellegen, who spoke very good French. He confided in me. He, too, had wanted to be a writer. He had begun drafting a memoir of his youth, the years when he'd lived an adventurous life in Africa and New Guinea and had sailed on a small boat, the *Tasmanian.* But he "wasn't cut out to wield a pen." He liked to philosophize. He told me that, in life, you must never listen to other people's advice. And that it's very hard to live with a woman. And that youth, fame, and health don't last—he should know. And other reflections that I don't recall.

I think he was fond of me. We were both tall, he six-foot-four, I six-foot-six. Every evening I brought him back to his room, guiding him by the arm, because of all the vodka he had drunk. He always said to me, in English, "Thank you, my son," before dropping to sleep like a stone.

Bella asked me to lend her some money because she'd just lost a bundle at poker. I still had four hundred thousand old francs of the six hundred I'd received for the screenplay. I gave her three-quarters of it. I was in love with her, having always had a soft spot for tiny brunettes with green eyes. But I was too shy to tell her.

Shooting was completed in three weeks. Rollner hadn't even bothered to go watch the "rushes" at a cinema in Hyères. He sent the sound engineer. He had asked me to "condense" the last forty pages of script so that he could "wrap up" the ending in three days. He couldn't stand any more. He dozed off from boredom between scenes.

He regained interest in his work only when they filmed the sequence in which this retort snapped like a banner: "One can be Jewish and still be a flying ace, mister." He had Tellegen do fifteen takes of that scene, but never managed to get it just right.

There was a small party to celebrate the end of filming. For the occasion, Stocklin flew in from Paris in a private plane that he piloted himself. He managed an aerobatic landing in front of the hotel, pipe between his teeth.

The mood that evening was lively. An August evening, redolent of pine and eucalyptus. Rollner seemed relieved to have brought the film to a successful conclusion.

They took a photo of the entire cast and crew, which I'd like to find again. I was between Bella and Tellegen. Tellegen drank like a fish. It was painful to watch. Bella whispered to me that she'd lost the money I lent her, but she swore to pay me back in Paris. She gave me her phone number: Auteuil oo-o8.

That evening, I took Rollner aside and asked when *Captain Van Mers* would be released.

His eyes were cloudy. He had drunk a fair amount himself.

"But it's never going to be released, old man," he said with a shrug.

Then he pulled me out of the lounge where we were all gathered. I helped him upstairs. He halted on the first landing. He fixed me with his cloudy gaze.

"Tell me, old man . . . I've never understood why they hired you for this screenplay. Are you related to Stocklin?"

"I . . . I don't think so," I said.

He smiled and patted my head with a paternal hand.

"Anyway . . . we're all related . . . The movies are just one big family . . ."

We started back up the stairs. He stumbled on every step.

"This film is a piece of crap . . ."

"You think so?" I said.

"Personally, I couldn't care less. I said all I had to say in this film. *All* of it."

He brought his face close to mine.

"You know . . . my little sentence . . ."

I steered him down the hallway. I opened the door to his room.

"It's too bad for you, Patrick," he said. "But as for me, I said all I had to say in this film. One single sentence . . ."

Suddenly, he spun toward the sink, bent over, and vomited. I waited in the doorway. He turned back toward me, ashen. He smiled.

"Forgive me. I'm sick as a dog. You should go back with the others."

I sat down in the middle of the hallway, near his door, thinking he might need me. I heard the crash of furniture falling over and the plaintive creak bedsprings make when someone collapses onto them. Silence. And then, this sentence, barely audible, that he murmured between clenched teeth:

"One can be Jewish and still be a flying ace, mister . . ."

VIII

My wife and I had arrived at Place Clemenceau in Biarritz. We left behind the manorlike Café Basque and headed down Avenue Victor-Hugo.

It was the start of a bright afternoon in early summer and a mild breeze was blowing. No pedestrians. The occasional car passed by, barely ruffling the silence. The market square and the churchyard of Saint-Joseph looked familiar. We passed through the doorway of the church. It was empty. A single candle was burning near the confessional. In whose name? I would have liked to consult the baptismal register, but seeing no one to ask, I thought we might come back later that afternoon.

We followed Avenue de la République. It hadn't changed much at all in twenty years and I stared at the building façades, hoping one of them would trigger a memory. It was as if we were strolling in the suburbs of Paris, in Jouy-en-Josas, for instance, in peaceful and mysterious Rue du Docteur-Kurzenne, where my brother and I had lived. But a house with more of a seaside-resort look to it than the others, bearing over its entrance the inscription "Villa Miramar" or "Villa Queen Nathalie," reminded me that we were in Biarritz. And the soft, clear light was that of the Côte d'Argent.

On Avenue de la République, children were heading into the Institut Sainte-Marie, a very old building whose façade had been repainted. The mesh fence was open and, after filing through it, they chased each other around the playground. A muffled ringing announced the start of class. And I remembered the morning in October 1950 when my mother and I walked across that yard and knocked at one of the French doors with gray wooden shutters. It was my first time at school and I was crying.

To our left, the narrow Friars Wynd stretched between two walls as far as the eye could see. I spotted a door that said: Institution de l'Immaculée Conception. To the right was a line of small villas. We reached the end of the avenue. There was a crossroads. A few more steps and, at the intersection of two streets, dominating the crossroads like a figurehead, stood Casa Montalvo.

How can I describe it? A massive edifice of pale stone, or rather a castle topped by a beveled slate roof. A very wide path led to the entrance door, which was sheltered by a slate awning. The lawn of Casa Montalvo was encircled by a high wall. I went through the white wooden gate but couldn't bring myself to walk to the entrance. At the end of the path, to the left, amid clumps of flowers, rose a palm tree that certainly impressed us when we were children, but that hadn't left the slightest trace in my memory. I tried to identify the windows of the small apartment where my brother Rudy and I lived, as Casa Montalvo was divided into several furnished units. From our windows, we could see the Chateau Grammont across the intersection, with its red brick façade in the style of Louis XIII, its turrets and neglected park.

I shut the gate behind me. On either side of it, a plaque. On the left-hand one, I read "Casa," and on the right, "Montalvo."

My wife stood waiting for me, smoking a cigarette. We walked straight ahead to Rue Saint-Martin, and soon we stopped at the church of the same name. I believe this church dates from the fifteenth century. We met a priest in a cassock, and I asked whether one could obtain a copy of a baptism certificate. He pointed me toward a small building opposite the church. We went inside. A rather elderly woman was sitting behind the window. My wife went to sit on a bench in the back of the room, and I, leaning toward the window, said:

"I've come to get a copy of a baptism certificate."

I was more and more convinced that the baptism had taken place in this church.

"On what date?" the old woman asked in a very soft voice.

"Oh . . . summer 1950."

And, saying "summer 1950," I felt a wave of sadness.

I spelled out my name, and she patiently combed through the register for the months of June, July, August, and September. She finally found it on September 24th.

"It was autumn 1950, not summer," she said with a wan smile.

She made a copy of the baptismal record and handed me the sheet, which read:

CERTIFICATE OF BAPTISM

PARISH OF ST. MARTIN — BIARRITZ DIOCESE OF BAYONNE

Baptismal Register, Year 1950 — Certificate no. 145

On this date, September 24, 1950, was baptized: P

Born July 30, 1945, in Paris

Son of: A,

and of: L,

Permanent residence: 15 Quai de Conti, Paris.

Godfather: André Camoin, represented by J. Minthe and V. Rachevsky.

Godmother: Madeleine Ferragus.

Additional notes: None.

I carefully folded the duplicate baptism certificate and slid it into my inner jacket pocket. My wife and I left.

And so I had been baptized in this little church of Saint-Martin . . . I had a vague memory of the ceremony, of my apprehension when the priest led me toward the baptismal font, and of the group formed by my brother, baptized the day before, my mother, my god-mother, Madeleine Ferragus, and the two individuals "representing" my godfather. Only one clear image remained: of Rachevsky's large white convertible, parked in front of the church. A random baptism.

Whose idea was it? And why did we stay in Biarritz for almost a year, my brother and I? I think the Korean War might have had something to do with it: that because of it, with the previous war in mind, they had decided to keep us away from Paris and baptize us as a precaution. I remember something my father said, when he came to see us at Casa Montalvo before heading off to Africa: "If the war lasts much longer, I'll take you with me to Brazzaville." And on the world globe he had given us, he pointed out that city in French Equatorial Africa.

Other images . . . One night in Saint-Jean-de-Luz, at a *toro de fuego*, I hurled myself at someone who was tossing confetti at my mother. A van had knocked me down as I was leaving Sainte-Marie. The convent of Dominican nuns on Avenue de la République, which we had passed by earlier, where they had put me out with ether to tend to my injuries. The military fanfare that we listened to, my brother and I, beneath the trees in Place Pierre-Forsans.

At the end of Rue Saint-Martin, my wife and I followed Avenue J.-F.-Kennedy. Back then, it had had a different name. We sat at a sidewalk table of a small café, in the sun. Behind us, the owner and two others were discussing next Sunday's pelota match. Through the fabric of my jacket, I fingered the copy of my baptism certificate. Many things had changed since then, there had been quite a few sorrows, but it was nonetheless comforting to have found my old parish.

IX

Have I really changed so much since the time I lived in Lausanne, in the Canton of Vaud?

In the evening, when I left the Florimont School, I caught the subway that looks like a funicular and that, from the center of town, descends toward Ouchy. I didn't have to do much work at the Florimont School. Three French lessons a week, which I gave to foreign students, outside of their normal curriculum. Sort of like summer school. I dictated interminable texts to them, which they couldn't understand because of my muffled voice.

I was only twenty years old, but my memory stretched back before my birth. I was certain, for instance, that I'd lived in Paris under the Occupation because I recalled certain individuals from that time, as well as small, disturbing details that weren't in any history book. Still, I tried to fight the heaviness that pulled me backward, and dreamed of liberating myself from my poisoned memory. I would have given anything to be an amnesiac.

I thought about escaping to some lost island in the Indian Ocean, where my recollections of old Europe would pale into insignificance. Forgetfulness would soon follow. I would be cured. Instead, I settled on somewhere less distant that hadn't experienced the pains and torments of this century: Switzerland. I decided to stay there, for as long as my military deferment would allow.

My lessons at the Florimont School lasted until 7:15, and a kind of stupor that I still recall fondly would come over me on Avenue de Rumine. The apartment buildings and Municipal Theater were as lacking in relief as a trompe-l'oeil backdrop. On Place Saint-François stood a thirteenth-century church, which for me had no more reality than the unblemished façades of the bank buildings a bit farther on. Everything floated in Lausanne; one's gaze and one's heart slid by, unable to latch onto any kind of asperity. Everything was neutral. Neither time nor suffering had planted its leprosy here. Moreover, on this side of Lake Geneva, time had stopped centuries ago.

I often stopped at a café near Bel-Air Tower and listened in on the customers' conversations. Even their way of speaking French aggravated my overall sense of unreality. They had strange inflections, and French in their mouths became the language that filters through loudspeakers in international airports. The Vaudois accent seemed too heavy and rustic to be true.

I walked down to the platform of the Flon station. A subway station with no smell or sound, trains in sprightly colors like children's toys; we waited quietly for their doors to open. The cars glided in padded silence. Forehead pressed against the window, I stared at the neon advertisements. They looked very sharp — much sharper than in France — and shone in bright hues. Only they, and the lit station signs of Montriond and Jordils, could pierce my lethargy. I was happy. I had no more memory. My amnesia would thicken with each passing day, like a callus. No more past. No more future. Time would halt and everything would blend into the blue mist of Lake Geneva. I had reached the state I called "Switzerland of the heart."

It was a topic of friendly disagreement between me and Michel Muzzli, a Swiss boy my age whom I'd met at the beginning of my stay and who worked for an insurance company. He reproached me for having a false idea of his country, the sort of idea common among rich cosmopolitans who spend their sunset years around Montreux — or among political exiles. No, Switzerland was not the no-man's-land, the limbo that I wanted to see it as. Each time I spoke the words "Swiss neutrality," they provoked an obvious pain in Muzzli. He doubled over as if he'd been shot in the gut, and his face turned purple. In a staccato voice, he explained that "neutrality" did not correspond, in any deep sense, to what he called the "Swiss soul." Politicians, notables, and industrialists had done everything in their power to drag Switzerland onto the path of "neutrality," but from there to thinking that "they" expressed the country's aspirations . . . No, "they" had — according to Muzzli — diverted it from its true vocation, which was to assume and atone for all the world's sufferings and injustices. The Switzerland Muzzli dreamed about, which would soon be "revealed," took on in his mind the appearance of a pure, radiant young woman starting out on an adventure. She was constantly affronted, her white dress spattered, but through all the insults and mudslinging she persevered, smiling and merciful, and perhaps taking a certain sensual delight in her Stations of the Cross. This masochistic vision of Switzerland worried me somewhat, but Michel, when not speaking about his country, was the gentlest of souls. A rather tall blond, with prominent cheekbones, transparent blue eyes, and wispy mustache, who looked more Russian than Swiss.

He introduced me to another boy named Badrawi, whom we nicknamed Papou, and soon the three of us became inseparable. Badrawi held some mysterious job in a bank on Rue Centrale. He was of Egyptian origin and his family had left Alexandria after the downfall of King Farouk. His only remaining relative was an old aunt who lived in Geneva, to whom he sent half his salary. Very short and slight, with black eyes and hair, he had a child's laugh, but his gaze often bespoke a vague terror. He and Muzzli lived in the same modern building, on Chemin de Chandolin, near the Federal Courthouse. Papou Badrawi's room was crammed full of English books. On the nightstand was a photo of his fiancée, also English, a girl with a feline face who wrote him long letters to say that she loved him but was cheating on him, but it didn't matter because she loved him. This was not Papou's viewpoint. He talked to me about it a few times, as we drank tea. He consumed a lot of tea, and when you knocked at his door, you could expect to be greeted with a steaming cup of Earl Grey.

We all weathered difficult moments. Once or twice a month,

Muzzli made what we called a "ruckus." On those nights, the telephone in Papou's room would ring and someone would ask him to come pick up his friend, for Muzzli always carried Badrawi's number on him. The first few times, Muzzli had chosen as the site of his "ruckuses" a nightclub on Avenue Benjamin-Constant where he knew one of the emcees, a blonde who was the spitting image of the actress Martine Carol, and who in fact was named Micheline Carole. Then there was the restaurant in the Hôtel de la Paix. And the main hall of the train station. And the Municipal Theater, one evening when a troupe from Zurich was performing Schiller's *William Tell*. Before long people began recognizing him, and he was barred from entering public places.

One evening, at Badrawi's, we had been waiting for Michel for two or three hours when the phone rang: the manager of an "inn" warned us that "Monsieur Muzzli" was already in a "very bad way" and was about to get himself "lynched." He didn't want any "trouble with the police." Up to us to "get Monsieur Muzzli out of this mess." The inn was located about five miles away, in a village called Chalet à Gobet. We took a cab and wandered for some time before finding the establishment, in the middle of a small pine forest. Muzzli was lying on a table in the back of the room, face badly bruised and his shirt open. His left foot was missing its shoe. A group of about a dozen persons, who looked rural, gave us hostile glares. Muzzli let himself slide off the table and stumbled toward us. He had a split lip. Badrawi and I held him up by the arms and, as we were crossing the doorway into the fresh air, we heard someone at our backs shout in a very strong Vaud accent:

"Good thing they came to get 'im. Otherwise we'd a finished off the piece of crap . . ."

As usual, Muzzli had harangued them about Switzerland. I knew all his arguments by heart. He'd told them that Switzerland had been "asleep" since the turn of the century and that it was time for it to wake up and finally "get its hands dirty." Otherwise, the Swiss would look more and more like a bunch of "clean little pink piglets." That evening, they nearly *had* lynched him, but that was what he wanted: for someone to lynch him, Michel Muzzli, Swiss citizen, and ideally for it to happen in a slum amid heaps of trash. And so he would atone for his country's excessive cleanliness and other crimes.

While Michel aspired to be a martyr, Badrawi, on the contrary, lived in terror of being murdered. He confided this secret to me early in our friendship. He couldn't put out of his mind that his cousin, a certain Alec Scouffi, had been killed in Paris in 1932, in circumstances that remained murky. Scouffi was born in Alexandria and had published two novels in French and a biography of the singer Caruso. His photo had pride of place on my friend's nightstand, and the resemblance was so striking that for a long time I thought it was a photo of Badrawi himself. Sometimes I wondered whether he hadn't invented this cousin because he liked the idea of being murdered. Whatever the case, Papou was convinced that the same people who had killed his cousin would kill him as well, and no amount of reasoning or friendly persuasion could talk him out of it. He would admit only that he ran less risk in Switzerland than anywhere else. He was certain that Swiss neutrality would protect him like a veil and that no one would dare commit a murder in this country. Muzzli tried to convince him otherwise, and reproached him for hanging the portrait of General Henri Guisan on his wall. But Badrawi replied that the gentle, paternal face of that Swiss soldier, who had never fought and never killed anyone, was a great comfort to him and calmed his nerves.

And so, when night fell, we each returned to our solitude: Michel Muzzli to his regret at being Swiss, and Papou, his fear of assassination that made him bolt the door to his room and huddle on his bed with a cup of tea. As for me, I listened to the radio. By turning the dial a millimeter at a time—if the needle made too sudden a jump, I had to start over—I managed to pick up the station Genève-Variétés on the medium waves. At precisely 10 p.m., the program *Music in the Night* came on. Ever since I had discovered this nightly broadcast, which lasted only twenty minutes, I couldn't stop listening to it, alone in my room on Avenue d'Ouchy. A theme song picked out on the piano, its melody filled with tropical grace. A voice coming in over the theme, announcing in deep, slightly nasal tones:

"*Music in the Night.*"

Then another voice, more metallic:

"With your hosts . . ."

The first voice, deep as ever:

"Robert Gerbauld . . ."

The second voice, higher-pitched, almost feminine:

". . . and Jean-Xavier Curtine."

You heard the theme song for a few seconds more. After the final chord, the first voice, Gerbauld's, specified in a tone of furtive complicity:

"That was, as always, a piece by Heitor Villa-Lobos."

During the twenty minutes the program lasted, they announced sonatas, adagios, capriccios, and fantasias. They had a marked taste for composers of Spanish inspiration, and it was with a gourmand's inflections that Gerbauld pronounced the names Albéniz, Manuel de Falla, Granados . . . Neither of them added any commentary; they merely gave the title of the piece, which lent their show a dry elegance. At the end, quiet piano notes: the second theme. A final chord, barely perceptible. Then Gerbauld's voice:

"That was, as always, *Sonata No. 6 in D Major* by Hummel."

And the voice of Jean-Xavier Curtine, staccato but tender:

"Thank you, dear listeners, this has been *Music in the Night.* Good evening, and until tomorrow."

What happened to me after a few days, as I listened to that program? I don't know if my hearing had become more acute, but I thought I made out a slight crackling sound under the flow of music. At first I thought it was the static you get when you pick up a foreign channel, but I soon became convinced it was the murmur of several overlapping conversations, a confused murmur from which a voice occasionally emerged, sending out a call for help or a muddled dispatch, as if people were taking advantage of the program to exchange messages or grope their way toward each other. As if their voices were vainly trying to pierce the screen of the music. On other evenings, this didn't occur and the pieces that Gerbauld or Curtine announced played from start to finish with crystalline clarity.

One Sunday, it took me longer than usual to pick up Genève-Variétés. *Music in the Night* had already been on for ten minutes, and to my surprise, I heard Gerbauld say:

"Dear listeners"—and his voice had an uncharacteristic tremor—"the piece we've just heard has touched me deeply. This music is like a wail from beyond the grave, a long cry of exile . . ."

A pause. Gerbauld resumed, his voice still more shaken:

"The composer surely wished to express his feeling of being the last survivor of a vanished world, a ghost among ghosts."

Another silence. Then Curtine's voice, husky:

"That feeling is one you know all too well, Robert Gerbauld."

And Gerbauld's voice, abrupt, as if afraid the other would say too much: "Dear listeners, good evening. Until tomorrow."

One thought nailed me to the spot, provoked by the words I had just heard: *beyond the grave, exile, ghost among ghosts.* Robert Gerbauld reminded me of someone. I stretched out on the bed and stared at the wall in front of me. A face appeared amid the flowers of the wallpaper. A man's face. The face that emerged from the wall, plain to see, belonged to D., the most heinous figure in Occupied Paris; D., whom I knew to have hidden out in Madrid, then Switzerland, and who *was living under an assumed name in Geneva, having found work on the radio.* But of course: Robert Gerbauld—it was he. Once more, the past engulfed me. One night in March 1942, a man of barely thirty, tall, looking like he might be South American, happened to be in the Saint-Moritz, a restaurant on Rue Marignan, almost at the corner of Avenue des Champs-Elysées. This was my father.

A young woman was with him, named Hella Hartwich. Ten-thirty in the evening. A group of French police in plain clothes entered the restaurant and blocked all the exits. Then they began checking the diners' identities. My father and his girlfriend had no papers. The French police shoved them into the Black Maria with a dozen others for a more extensive check on Rue Greffulhe, at the headquarters of the Jewish Affairs Police.

When the Black Maria turned into Rue Greffulhe, my father noticed that people were coming out of the Mathurins theater, where they were playing *Mademoiselle from Panama*. The inspectors dragged them into what had been a living room. It still had the chandelier and the mirror above the mantelpiece. In the middle of the room was a large, light-colored wooden desk, behind which was a man in an overcoat, whose fleshy, clean-shaven face my father remembered. That was D.

He asked my father and his girlfriend for their names. Out of lassitude or defiance, they gave them. D. absently leafed through several sheets of paper, on which were no doubt listed all the names that sounded suspicious. He raised his head and signaled to one of his men.

"Take them to the holding tank."

In the stairway, my father, his girlfriend, and three or four other suspects were bookended by two inspectors. The hallway light went out. Before anyone could turn it back on, my father, pulling his girlfriend with him, hurtled down the flight of stairs between him and the ground floor and they fled through the street entrance. They ran toward Rue des Mathurins. They thought they heard shouts and the sound of footsteps behind them. Then the engine of the Black Maria. They skirted Square Louis-XVI, pushed open the door to a building, and flew up the staircase in the dark. They reached the top floor without attracting attention. There, they waited for morning. They had no idea what they'd just avoided. After the holding tank came the camps at Drancy or Compiègne. And after that, the deportation convoys. A flat, ridgeless face. A mouth with a rimmed, drooping upper lip and a minuscule lower lip, and that mouth was the same as on certain frogs that glue their faces to the glass of aquariums. Skin that was olive, smooth, and lacking in any body hair. That was how D. appeared to me that night, he who moved in and out of black market restaurants under the Occupation, surrounded by a gang of ephebes, part killers, part boy scouts, whom oddly enough they used to call the Gray Gloves. D., the man on Rue Greffulhe. He followed me even to this land where I'd thought I would gradually discard my memory. His head glided along the wall, floating closer, and already I could feel his clammy, flaccid touch.

And yet, how beautiful life was that spring . . . In the hours of freedom that our jobs left us, we arranged to meet up, Papou, Muzzli, and I, by the side of a small swimming pool at a hotel on the corner of Avenue d'Ouchy and Avenue de Cour. It was built at the back of a garden and sheltered from Avenue d'Ouchy by a curtain of trees. Micheline Carole would come join us when she got up, at around one. She sunbathed all afternoon long, as her job didn't start until evening. Two twin sisters were also part of our gang, two tiny, gorgeous Indonesians, who claimed to be "studying" in Lausanne.

On the pale green water floated children's life preservers bearing the inscription "Happy Days," followed by the number of that year. 1965? 1966? 1967? What difference does it make? I was twenty.

Then some very strange coincidences occurred. One Saturday morning, I went to the pool earlier than usual. A swimmer who had arrived before me was doing the butterfly stroke. When he saw me, he rushed over and we hugged: it was a friend from Paris, a young Belgian singer named Henri Seroka. He was living in that hotel. He had competed, he told me, in a singing contest in Evian, and since the Evian hotels were full, the contest organizers had found him a room in Lausanne. The elimination rounds had lasted five days, and every morning he took the boat that shuttled between Lausanne and Evian.

The jury had selected him for the semifinals, then eliminated him in the last round, despite "popular demand." His defeat didn't seem to bother him. He had been there for a week and couldn't bring himself to leave the hotel. Even he was surprised by the indolence and torpor slowly taking hold of him. He didn't even care about his bill, which grew larger with each passing day and which he couldn't afford to pay. We were happy to see each other. Henri Seroka brought me back to a past that was still recent, to afternoons when my friend Hughes de Courson and I would hang around the shabby offices of Fantasia Music on Rue de Grammont. We wrote songs and Seroka had recorded one of them, "Les oiseaux reviennent," which earned him an honorable mention at the Sopot Festival and a medal at the Grand Competition of Song in Barcelona. Since then, Fantasia Music had foundered and many people we knew had gone down with it, but it was sweet to run into each other by this pool.

We had a few days' vacation for Pentecost, and it felt as if we all forgot our cares. Michel Muzzli was relaxed, and there wasn't a single "ruckus." I was hoping he'd finally made his peace with his homeland. Badrawi regained an Eastern insouciance under the warm sun and fretted less about assassination. And besides, his English fiancée had written, asking to visit him in Lausanne the following month. As for Henri Seroka, he spoke without bitterness of the Evian competition. He'd been narrowly edged out by a thirteen-year-old prodigy who had appeared onstage in short pants, white shirt, and tie to sing some rock 'n' roll numbers. Even Seroka couldn't help laughing. He really didn't know what demon had pushed him to compete in that stupid contest. He couldn't resist. Whenever he heard about a singing competition, he entered it, and so had taken some lovely trips, not only to Sopot, Poland, but also to Italy, Austria, and the USSR. They were getting to know him on the other side of the Iron Curtain. He had sung in Moscow, Leningrad, and Kiev, and there, he said, he had met his true audience. I didn't doubt it. More than anyone, the Russians must have appreciated his classic crooner's voice as well as his classic physique: he was the spitting image of Errol Flynn. More-over, Micheline Carole seemed increasingly susceptible to his charm. It was mutual. In the middle of the pool, they indulged in a kind of aquatic flirtation. The couple they formed—he, the double of Errol Flynn; she, of Martine Carol—gave me the illusion that time had flowed back to the source. Those two deceased actors were here with us again, as in the halcyon days of our childhood, and were even kind enough to swim and flirt before my half-closed eyes.

One of the tiny Indonesians took a shine to me, while her twin sister found Muzzli appealing. Papou Badrawi, nestled deep in his deck chair, dreamed about the arrival of his fiancée. We all floated in a sensual mist, heightened by the sun's reflections on the green water, the quivering of the trees along Avenue d'Ouchy, and the Pimp's champagne that Seroka ordered for us. Our get-togethers lasted until very late, and I no longer had a chance to tune in to *Music in the Night*.

Yes, there are some very odd coincidences. I was distractedly leafing through a Swiss newspaper by the side of the pool when my eye fell on this notice: "Starting tomorrow, the outdoor theater in Lausanne will present a program of music from the French Riviera. Founded three years ago by former students of Prof. Ansermet, it brings together numerous musicologists, among them our colleagues from Genève-Variétés, Robert Gerbauld and Jean-Xavier Curtine."

I stood up, put on a white terrycloth robe, and left the others. I followed the gravel path that led from the pool to the hotel. I was certain I'd already lived through this day. I could also foretell the rest, as in a dream when you know that the blonde Countess du Barry will be guillotined, but when you try to warn her and urge her to flee Paris in time, she just shrugs.

I went up to the reception desk and asked the man on duty:

"Has Monsieur Gerbauld arrived yet?"

"He's at the bar, sir."

I was expecting that. I could even have prompted him.

"At the bar, sir . . ."

He stretched out his arm to show me the entrance to the bar.

I remained on the threshold of the bar, a large room with light-colored wood paneling, a coffered ceiling, and low tables surrounded by plaid-upholstered armchairs.

I recognized him right off. He was sitting to the right of the entrance, facing the other one. They were chatting. A smell of incense paper hovered in the air, and I recalled effortlessly that this was his cologne. With a step that I labored to make natural—I was barefoot and afraid my bathrobe would draw their attention—I went to sit at a table a certain distance from theirs. They didn't notice me, being wholly absorbed in their conversation. They spoke loudly, Gerbauld in his warm voice, the other, the young one, in a tone even more metallic than on the radio.

"You know the problem as well as I do, Jean-Xavier," said Gerbauld.

"Of course."

"There's only one thing left for me to do."

"What's that?"

"Put their backs against the wall. Either a Manuel de Falla Festival next year, or a Hindemith Festival. End of story."

"You're going to tell them that?"

"If they refuse, I quit."

"Would you really, Robert?"

And so, right near me, sat the man who had been responsible for several thousand deportations in the years 1940 to 1944, the one who directed the "squads" of Rue de Greffulhe, from whom my father had miraculously escaped . . . I knew his pedigree. Unremarkable small-time lawyer before the war, then local councilor; he had added a nobiliary "de" to his name and founded the Anti-Jewish Rally. At the Liberation, he had taken refuge in Madrid, where, under the name

Estève, he had taught French. I knew everything about him, down to his date of birth: March 23, 1901, in Cahors.

"... A Manuel de Falla Festival, or no festival at all!"

"It's really amazing how unfair those people are to de Falla," Jean-Xavier noted pensively.

"Unfair or not, I'll slam the door right in their faces!"

So that person a few feet away from me would rather I'd never been born? I looked at him with extreme curiosity. The photo I'd clipped from a Liberation newspaper was not very sharp, owing to the poor-quality paper, but I could tell his face had puffed up in twenty-five years—especially his jowls—and that he'd lost his hair. He was wearing glasses with gold frames and stems. He smoked a pipe, which he kept in his mouth even while speaking, and it gave him a placid air that surprised me. His bald skull and his corpulence exuded affability. He was wearing a black velvet suit and a burgundy turtleneck pullover. A fat clergyman. The other one, Jean-Xavier Curtine, was nothing more than a young man with regular features, but with a very narrow face and pale complexion. His dark hair looked like it was shellacked in place. His tight, peacock-blue suit, his signet ring, his precise little gestures, his moccasins—all of it suggested an Asian meticulousness. Moreover, he might have been Eurasian.

"So, do you think they'll go for the Manuel de Falla Festival?"

Gerbauld nibbled on his pipe.

"Naturally ..."

He smiled, pipe between his teeth.

"Especially if I promise to air the whole thing on Genève-Variétés ..."

"It would be marvelous," said Curtine in his metallic insect voice, "if we could have them play de Falla's *Atlántida*."

Gerbault nodded, pensive.

"Yes, yes, yes ..."

At that moment, the bartender approached their table.

"Would the gentlemen care for anything?"

"I'll have a beer," said Gerbauld. "Draft. What about you?"

"A grenadine . . ."

Then the bartender came to my table.

"A Suze," I said.

They had noticed my presence and both of them looked at me, no doubt surprised by my pool attire. Gerbauld smiled. He gave me a friendly nod, to which I responded. Our drinks were served.

"How is it?" Gerbauld asked, facing in my general direction.

"How's what?"

"The water in the pool."

"Very nice."

He turned to Curtine.

"You should go swimming, Jean-Xavier. That fellow says it's nice."

"I plan to," the other said, smiling at me.

"Cheers," Gerbauld said to me, raising his glass of beer.

I grimaced a smile, then stood up and left the bar.

I crossed the lobby with huge strides and ran down the gravel path to the pool.

Muzzli and Papou were swimming. Henri Seroka was lying next to Micheline Carole on a large red-and-white beach towel. They were holding hands.

"Where did you go?" he asked.

What could I say? They told me that Hedy, the Indonesian girl, had been looking for me for the past half-hour.

Muzzli and Papou came out of the pool and joined us.

"You look pale," observed Seroka. "You should have a Porto flip."

I was shaking, but I tried to hold my body stiff so they wouldn't notice.

"Are you okay?" asked Muzzli.

"Yes, yes, I'm fine. Just fine."

I slipped off my bathrobe and dove in. I remained for a long time underwater, eyes open. As long as I could. An eternity. When I resurfaced, I rested my elbows on the edge of the pool and leaned my chin on the blue mosaic.

"It's nice, isn't it?" said Seroka. "I'll order you a Porto flip."

Two men were walking on the path, farther on, coming toward us, closer and closer. Curtine and Gerbauld. Curtine was wearing a light-blue bathing suit with V-shaped notches on the hips. Gerbauld had kept his black velvet suit and was carrying a camera of impressive size, slung over his shoulder.

They stopped across the pool from us. Gerbauld sat on the one canvas chair and Curtine squatted near him. His bearing was fairly athletic, like people of small stature who take an exaggerated interest in building their muscles. With a sudden jerk, he stood up and went to test the water with his left foot. He remained poised for a few seconds, right leg slightly bent, left leg stiff like a dancer en pointe, torso very straight, arms behind his back. Without getting up, Gerbauld had trained his lens on Curtine and was pressing the shutter. Curtine smiled.

My friends and I watched them, and I noticed a certain interest among Seroka, Micheline Carole, and Badrawi. I was seized with an urge to call out to Gerbauld by his real name, but the place wasn't right and I was afraid I'd scare the others. Curtine walked with slow, supple steps to the diving board. He made it bend several times, jumping very high, as if testing out its elasticity. Gerbauld had gotten up from the canvas chair and, from a standing position, continued to photograph Curtine.

Finally, Curtine executed an elegant dive and, after several strokes, snorted and hoisted himself onto the pool edge with a single pull of his arms. Again Gerbauld photographed him, but this time from up close. He slung his camera back across his chest, picked up a large red-and-white towel draped over the back of the chair, unfolded it, wrapped it around Curtine, and massaged his shoulders with the kinds of firm, protective motions that a trainer might use on his star boxer. Curtine lay back flat on the ground, legs tight, abdominal muscles visibly tensed. He kept stroking his hair with his hands to brush it back. Gerbauld knelt beside him, aimed his camera, and shot again.

"How was it?" he asked.

"Very nice."

They lowered their voices, and I couldn't hear what they were saying. Then Gerbauld raised his eyes and looked across the pool.

He saw me and waved.

"You know that guy?" Badrawi asked.

"No."

After about fifteen minutes, they got up, Curtine wrapped in his red-and-white beach towel that he dropped negligently by the side of the pool. He walked toward the path, advancing in small strides, like an athlete taking to the podium during a bodybuilding contest. He walked on tiptoe so as not to lose a centimeter of his small height. Gerbauld followed behind, slightly hunched. Passing by where we were, Curtine turned and said to me:

"It was very nice. Very nice. Thank you."

Again I smelled that odor of incense paper. Then the two of them disappeared down the path toward the hotel.

"Odd ducks," said Seroka.

We went to have lunch at the sidewalk of a restaurant across the avenue, near the Ouchy church. I found Hedy, the Indonesian, who asked me to come to her place. Hedy shared with her twin sister a room on the ground floor of a building near Jordils station; from their window, you could see, at the foot of a small valley, the sprightly colored trains heading down to Ouchy.

I felt a kind of relief when I entered that white room, which had no furnishings or wall hangings. A large mattress on the floor, a light bulb hanging from the ceiling, and that was it. Neutral, like Switzerland.

I asked to make a phone call. She didn't seem to mind. She spoke no French, so we communicated in very approximate English. Besides, we didn't need to speak. I dialed the number of the hotel.

"Robert Gerbauld, please . . ."

A click. Gerbauld's deep voice:

"Yes, hello?"

"Is this Robert Gerbauld?"

"It is."

"I'm a faithful listener to *Music in the Night*."

A pause. Then I heard him say in a tone of forced cheerfulness:

"Ah, I see. And how did you know I was here?"

"I'm going to the music festival."

"Ah, I see . . ."

"I'd very much like to meet you. I'm a young admirer . . ."

"How old are you?"

"Eighteen. Couldn't I meet you, Monsieur Gerbauld? Even for just five minutes . . ."

"Well . . . you're catching me a little off-guard . . ."

"It would make me so happy."

A pause. Under his breath, as if he didn't want someone nearby, perhaps Curtine, to overhear:

"We could try to meet for a moment this evening . . ."

"Yes."

In a voice that was still lower and more rushed:

"Listen . . . the café on Avenue d'Ouchy . . . Opposite the main entrance of the Beaurivage hotel . . . Eight-thirty . . . Good-bye for now."

He hung up.

The Indonesian girl and I stayed in that smooth white room until five in the afternoon. Then we joined the others and went swimming with Micheline Carole and Henri Seroka. Badrawi, sprawled on an inflatable mattress, was doing a crossword puzzle. A bit farther on, beneath the trees, Michel Muzzli was chatting with the other Indonesian, Hedy's twin sister. I watched the tiny buoys dancing on the surface of the water.

Henri Seroka ordered us aperitifs, and in an anisette fog we made our plans for the evening. Badrawi invited us to dinner. At eight-fifteen, I asked him to drop me off at the café on Avenue d'Ouchy where Gerbauld had set our rendezvous. We'd come back to pick up the others at the hotel bar.

"Do you have a pressing engagement?" he asked, a curious look in his eye.

"Yes. Crucial."

Muzzli and the other Indonesian girl came with us. Badrawi drove his old Peugeot slowly. I told Papou to stop at the end of the road that led to the Beaurivage.

By the way, would they mind if I brought someone else with us in the car? Afterward, we'd take him somewhere isolated. They suddenly seemed nervous. The Indonesian girl looked at us one after the other, not understanding. I told them some details about Gerbauld.

"You're not really thinking of killing him, are you?" said Muzzli.

"No."

At exactly eight-thirty, I saw Gerbauld on the left-hand sidewalk of the avenue. He was walking quickly toward the café. He was wearing a beige linen suit and a hat that was also made of beige linen, shaped like one of those Tyrolean hats. He slipped quickly into the café.

I couldn't make myself leave the car seat. Muzzli turned to me.

"Isn't that the guy from the pool?"

I didn't answer. All I had to do was cross the avenue and follow him into the café. I would have shaken his hand, we would have ordered two beers, and we would have talked about Manuel de Falla. I would have offered to drive him back to the hotel. He would have gotten into the Peugeot and Badrawi would have started up. No, I didn't want to kill him, but I did want to have a "discussion."

"Shall we wait?" asked Badrawi.

"Yes."

Not even a "discussion." A few words that I would have whispered to him before we parted company at the entrance of his hotel:

"Still at Rue Greffulhe?"

He would have gaped at me with the terrified look that people get when you remind them, point-blank, of some trivial detail from their past. The dress or shoes they wore on such-and-such an evening. How could you know that? You weren't born yet. That's incredible. You're frightening me.

Night. Muzzli had switched on the radio. Badrawi was smoking and the Indonesian girl sat next to me, impassive and silent. I saw him leave the café. He paused on the sidewalk, looked left, then right. The neon shone pink on him. He had taken off his hat and was staring at the tips of his shoes; he looked tired. He raised his head and I was surprised to see that his features had gone gaunt, no doubt because of the darkness and the neon glow. I hadn't noticed, in the bar and at the pool, his prominent chin, nor his sinuous mouth that gave him the face of a frog, as in my dreams.

Supposing it really was D. — and I was less and less certain — I knew in advance that, hearing my little utterance, he would look at me with glazed eyes. It would mean nothing to him anymore. Memory itself is corroded by acid, and of all those cries of suffering and horrified faces from the past, only echoes remain, growing fainter and fainter, vague outlines. Switzerland of the heart.

He had donned his Tyrolean-style hat and, with it on, he looked like a toad whose head peers out steadily from a lily pad. He stood there, motionless, under the neon lights. I didn't dare ask Papou or Michel whether they saw the same thing I did, or just a poor old queen waiting on the sidewalk after being stood up.

A mirage, no doubt. Besides, it was all a mirage; everything in this country was devoid of reality. We were kept apart, as Muzzli said, from the "sufferings of the world." There was nothing left but to let ourselves be engulfed by the lethargy that I persisted in calling "Switzerland of the heart."

There, across from us, on the other side of the avenue, he looked left and right, standing stiffly under the pink light. He took his pipe from his pocket and contemplated it.

"Shall we go join the others?" I said to Badrawi.

X

It was in the Luxembourg Gardens, one winter morning ten years ago, that I learned of Fats's death. I had pulled up a metal chair next to the pond and unfolded the newspaper. A picture of Fats— mustache, dark glasses, white silk scarf, and the felt hat he often wore to go out—accompanied the article. He had keeled over in a restaurant on the Viale Trastevere, probably while eating a dish of that green lasagna he loved so well.

I was eighteen, working in a bookstore in Rome, when I was introduced to Fats by a French girl a bit older than I who performed at the Open Gate, a cabaret on Via San Niccolò da Tolentino. A brunette, with slanted eyes and a lovely, candid mouth, called Claude Chevreuse, at least professionally. At around midnight she would appear onstage wearing a mink coat and evening gown and begin a languid striptease while the piano man played the theme from *They Shall Have Music*. Two white toy poodles capered around her, turning somersaults in the air, and snatched her stockings, bra, garters, and panties between their teeth as she peeled them off. For some time, Fats had been a regular presence in the audience, always on his own, and when Claude returned to her dressing room, she would find a rose from this nightly spectator.

Fats invited us to his table one night after the show. When Claude introduced us, he burst into a guffaw that jiggled his shoulders and flabby cheeks. I happened to have the same name as a brand of cards that everyone in Italy used for playing poker. Fats found this riotously funny, and from then on his nickname for me was Poker.

That evening, after we'd had a last drink at a sidewalk café on the

Via Veneto, Claude whispered in my ear that she had to go home with Fats. They climbed into a cab in front of the Excelsior. Fats lowered the window, waved his stubby fingers, and said, "Arrivederla, Poker."

I felt a twinge to think that Claude had abandoned me, yet again, for someone who was hardly worth it. I don't know why I loved that girl from Chambéry, who had come to Rome a few years back to "make a name in the movies." Since then, she had let herself go, started doing a bit of cocaine. In Rome, things tend to end rather than begin.

From then on, I would run into Fats at the Open Gate whenever I went to pick up Claude Chevreuse. He waited for her in her dressing room. She treated him cruelly and made cutting remarks about his weight, but Fats didn't respond, or just nodded. One evening, she deserted us both on the Via Veneto, saying she had a date with a "very attractive, very slim" boy, stressing the word "slim" to needle Fats. We watched her leave, then went to get pastries. I tried to distract Fats, who seemed utterly dejected. I suppose that's why he came to like me, and why we got together again a dozen or so times. He would make appointments with me for four o'clock sharp at a small bar on Via delle Botteghe Oscure, and there he had what he called his "snack": about a dozen smoked-salmon sandwiches. Or else, in the evening, he took me to a restaurant near the Quirinale, where the coat-check lady greeted him as "Your Highness."

Fats, head bowed, absorbed huge plates of green lasagna; then he heaved a sigh as he fell back in his chair, and immediately sank into a vacant stupor. At around one in the morning, I tapped him on the shoulder and we went home.

We took walks together. A taxi dropped us off at Piazza Albania and we climbed up the Aventine Hill. It was one of the places in Rome that Fats liked best, "because of the quiet," he said. He would peer through the keyhole of the Knights of Malta Priory, beyond which you could spy the dome of St. Peter's in the distance, and burst into hysterical laughter that always astounded me.

I never dared bring up his past, or the details that had helped forge his legend: breaking the bank in Deauville and Monte Carlo, his collections of toys, stamps, and old telephones, or his taste for phosphorescent ties, on which a naked woman appeared if you shimmied the fabric. Still, one evening at the restaurant, as he was wolfing down his lasagna, I said it was a shame to end up this way, after so many good fairies had watched over his crib.

He looked up and gazed at me through his opaque lenses. He told me he remembered the exact moment when he had decided to give up and let himself gain weight, feeling that "nothing mattered a damn" and that he'd wind up the same as Louis XVI, Nicholas Romanov, and Maximilian, the ill-starred emperor of Mexico. It was one night in 1942, in Egypt. Rommel's forces were closing in from Cairo and a blackout enveloped the city. Fats sneaked into the Hotel Semiramis, incognito, and groped his way toward the bar. Not a glimmer of light. He stumbled against an armchair and fell on his back. And there, alone on the floor, in the dark, he was seized by wild, nervous laughter. He couldn't stop laughing. That instant marked the beginning of his decline.

It was the only time he opened up to me. Now and then, he might speak Claude Chevreuse's name. But that was all.

He invited us to his place for New Year's Eve. He lived in a tiny apartment in a modern building in the Parioli neighborhood. He opened the door. He was wearing a frayed blue velvet dressing gown, with his first initial and the crown of his defunct kingdom embroidered on the pocket. He looked distraught when he realized Claude Chevreuse wasn't with me. I told him that the show at the Open Gate would run longer than usual and Claude would be joining us very late.

In the small space with bare walls that served as his living room, Fats had set up a buffet: pastries, smoked-salmon sandwiches, and fruit. I noticed an old film projector on a barstool. It surprised me, but I didn't ask any questions, for I already knew he wouldn't answer.

He was glancing at his watch and perspiring.

"Do you think she'll come, Poker?"

"Yes, yes, of course. Not to worry."

"It's midnight, Poker. Happy New Year."

"Happy New Year to you, sir."

"Do you really think she'll come?"

He gobbled down sandwich after sandwich to allay his anxiety. Then the pastries. Then the fruit. He collapsed onto a chair, took off his dark glasses, put on a pair with lightly tinted lenses and gold frames. He stared at me through dull eyes.

"Poker, you're a nice boy. I feel like adopting you. What do you say?"

It seemed to me his eyes were misting up.

"I'm so lonely, Poker . . . But before adopting you, maybe I can bestow a title. How'd you like to be a bey? That all right?"

He bowed his head and we kept silent. I should have said thank you.

"Would you like me to read your cards, Poker?"

He took a deck of cards from the pocket of his gown and shuffled them. He was just starting to lay them out on the floor when we heard the doorbell buzz three times. It was Claude Chevreuse.

"Happy New Year! Buon anno! Auguri!" she cried, pacing back and forth across the living room in a state of excitement.

She was wearing her fake fur coat from the show. She hadn't had time to remove her makeup and was in a very merry mood, from drinking champagne with friends. She kissed Fats on the forehead and both cheeks, leaving lipstick traces.

"What say we all go out? We'll dance the night away!" she said. "I want to go to the Piccolo Siam . . ."

"First I'd like to show you a film," Fats announced in a sober voice.

"No, no, let's go out now! Let's go right now! I want to go to the Piccolo Siam!"

She tried to push Fats toward the door, but he held her back and made her sit in one of the chairs.

"I'd like to show you a film," he repeated.

"A film?" said Claude. "A film? He's out of his mind!"

He turned off the lights and started up the projector. Claude shrieked with laughter. She turned toward me and undid her fake fur. She had nothing on but panties.

On the wall opposite us, the images were fuzzy at first, then came into focus. It was an old newsreel from at least thirty years before. A very handsome, very slim, very earnest young man was standing on the prow of a warship that was slowly entering the port of Alexandria. A huge crowd had swarmed into the harbor and we could see thousands upon thousands of waving arms. The ship berthed and the young man waved his arm back at the crowd. They broke through the police barriers and invaded the docks, and all those ecstatic faces were turned toward the young man on the ship. He couldn't have been more than sixteen, his father had just passed away, and as of the previous day he was king of Egypt. He seemed moved and intimidated by the fervor that rose toward him, the rapturous crowd, the city festooned. Everything was about to begin. The future shone bright. That young man, in all his promise, was Fats.

Claude yawned—champagne always made her sleepy. I turned toward Fats, who was sitting to the right of the projector that was sputtering like a machine gun. With his glasses, his puffy face, and his mustache, he looked fatter and more apathetic than ever.

XI

Another time, one Saturday evening in June, I left Paris with my Uncle Alex. We were in one of those Citroëns called a DS 19, and my uncle was driving. I was fourteen. We had taken the Western high-way. On the unfolded map, I made a blue pencil X on the places we passed by. Since then, I've lost track of that map, and today I remember only one small town we passed through: Gisors. Was the property my Uncle Alex told me about located in the Eure or the Oise? An old mill up for sale at a "very attractive" price. My uncle had learned about it through a newspaper ad that he recited for me: "Charming mill all mod cons. Magnificent walled garden. River and orchard. Gorgeous village for outings." He had gotten in touch with the man handling the sale, a local notary.

Night was falling when we saw the sign for the inn, and we followed the arrow onto a side road. A grand-looking inn in Anglo-Norman style. The dining room extended onto a terrace with a swimming pool next to it. There were stained-glass windows with multicolored diamond shapes, Louis XV pedestal tables, and wood paneling. No other diners, as it was still early. My Uncle Alex ordered two galantines, two haunches of venison, and a renowned Burgundy. The wine steward had him taste it. Uncle Alex took a large mouthful, puffed up his cheeks, and looked as if he were gargling. Finally he said:

"It's nice . . . it's nice . . . But not silky enough."

"I beg your pardon?" said the steward, knitting his brow.

"Not silky enough," repeated Uncle Alex with much less assurance.

And in an abrupt tone:

"But fine, it will do."

When the steward left, I asked Uncle Alex:

"Why did you say it wasn't 'silky enough'?"

"It's a term of the trade. He doesn't know squat about wine."

"And you do?"

"A fair amount."

No, he didn't know anything. He never drank.

"I could teach those pissant sommeliers a thing or two."

He was shaking.

"Calm down, Uncle Alex," I said.

And he got his smile back. He mumbled some excuse for my benefit. We finished our desserts—two tartes Tatin—and Uncle Alex said to me:

"You know, we've never really talked before, just the two of us."

I sensed he wanted to confide in me. He tried to find the words.

"I feel like making a change."

He'd taken on an uncharacteristically serious tone. I folded my arms to show that I was giving him my full attention.

"My dear Patrick . . . There comes a time when you have to take stock . . ."

I gave a small nod of agreement.

"You have to start fresh, on solid ground, you understand?"

"Yes."

"You have to find your roots, you understand?"

"Yes."

"You can't keep being a man from nowhere."

He had given the syllables of "nowhere" a coquettish emphasis.

"A man from nowhere . . ."

And he pointed to himself with his left hand, bowing his head with an ingratiating half-smile. Once upon a time, it must have had quite an effect on the ladies.

"Your father and I are men from nowhere, you understand?"

"Yes."

"Did you know we don't even have birth certificates . . . a civil status record . . . like everyone else?"

"Not even that?"

"It can't go on like this. I've been mulling it over, and I'm convinced I'm right in having made this important decision."

"What decision, Uncle Alex?"

"My boy, it's very simple. I have decided to leave Paris and live in the country. I've been thinking a lot about that mill."

"You're going to buy it?"

"Very likely I will. I need to live in the country . . . I need to feel the earth and grass beneath my feet . . . It's time, Patrick."

"That sounds lovely, Uncle Alex."

He himself was moved by what he had just said.

"The country is a great place to start over. Do you know what I dream about every night?"

"No."

"A small village."

A shadow of worry darkened his eyes.

"Do you think I look French enough? Tell me the truth."

His black hair was brushed off his forehead; he had a wispy mustache, dark eyes, and very long eyelashes.

"What does that mean, to look French?" I asked.

"Good question . . ."

He pensively twirled his demitasse spoon in his cup.

"I've been thinking about your future, my dear Patrick," he said. "I think I've found the perfect profession for you."

"Have you?"

He lit a cigarette.

"A secure profession, because you never know what can happen in times like ours . . . It's important that you avoid the mistakes your father and I made . . . We were on our own. We had no one to guide us. We wasted a lot of time . . . I'm going to take the liberty of giving you advice, my dear Patrick . . . Shall I tell you the profession?"

He laid a hand on my shoulder. He looked me deep in the eyes, and in a solemn, husky voice, he said:

"You should go into the lumber trade, Patrick. I can give you a pamphlet about it. What do you think?"

"I'll have to let the idea sink in."

"Read the pamphlet. We'll talk some more."

Uncle Alex had ordered an herb tea, which he drank in small sips.

"I wonder what that mill is like. Do you think they've kept the millstone?"

He must have been dreaming about this for days. The word "mill" set me dreaming as well. I could hear the sound of the water, picture a stream flowing through the wild grasses.

The wine steward approached our table. He made an embarrassed motion and coughed to attract Uncle Alex's attention.

"Sir . . ." he finally said.

I tapped Uncle Alex on the shoulder.

"The gentleman would like to speak to you, Uncle Alex."

Uncle Alex looked up at the steward.

"Yes, what is it?"

"Sir, I'd like to ask you for something . . ."

He blushed and lowered his eyes.

"What?"

"An autograph, sir."

Uncle Alex stared at him, wide-eyed.

"You *are* the actor Gregory Ratoff, aren't you?"

My Uncle Alex bolted up, his face purple.

"Certainly not, sir. I am French and my name is François Aubert."

The other had a timid smile.

"No, sir. You are Gregory Ratoff . . . The Russian actor."

My Uncle Alex pulled me along by the arm. We fled through the dining room and the bar. The steward pursued us.

"Please, Monsieur Ratoff . . . Just an autograph, Monsieur Ratoff . . ."

The bartender, intrigued, walked toward the steward making a questioning gesture.

"He's a Russian actor . . . Gregory Ratoff . . ."

We had started up the stairs. With Uncle Alex pushing me, we climbed them four at a time. I stumbled and just managed to catch the railing. The other two were down below, looking up. They were waving.

"Monsieur Ratoff! . . . Monsieur Ratoff! . . . Monsieur Ratoff! . . ."

Uncle Alex collapsed onto one of the twin beds in our room. He closed his eyes.

"My name is François Aubert . . . François Aubert . . . Aubert . . ."

That night he slept poorly.

We had taken a wrong turn and arrived only at around noon in the village whose name I'd so like to recall. For these past fifteen years, I've scrutinized maps of the Eure, the Oise, and even the Orne regions, hoping to come across it. It was—I think—a melodious name ending in "-euil," something like Vainteuil, or Verneuil, or Septeuil.

A small village whose main road was still paved as in olden times. The houses that bordered it, mostly farms, gave off an impression of calm and solidity. It was a beautiful day. An old man, sitting on the steps of the local café, swiveled his head to watch our car pass by.

My Uncle Alex was sorry we'd wasted a night in that inn. We should have made the trip in one go. The appointment with the notary had been set for eleven, and the man must be getting impatient. No, you don't think so? We arrived at the square just as Mass was letting out, and we labored to look natural in our big fat automobile, while the crowd of worshipers flowed on either side of the DS 19 and stared in at us. Uncle Alex lowered his head. And suddenly, a projectile crashed against our windshield, which at its center was nothing more than glass dust, its specks holding together by a miracle.

"Just some kid messing around with his slingshot," I told Uncle Alex.

"You really think it's just a kid?"

We waited until everyone had left the square before getting out of the car. Uncle Alex locked the doors. He squeezed my arm, which was unusual and betrayed a deep anxiety. It didn't take us long to find Rue Bunau-Varilla, where the notary was waiting for us, at number 8. A very short man, bald, sixtyish and affable. He was wearing—why did this strike me? and why do I always remember such precise and pointless details?—a glen plaid suit of very ample cut. His gaze filtered through squinting eyelids, as if through venetian blinds.

"Shall we go see the mill?" he said to my uncle. "I think you'll like it. Personally, I'd be thrilled if you did."

We got back into the DS 19, Uncle Alex and the notary in front, me in back. Uncle Alex drove blind, because of the shattered windshield.

"Was it a bird that did that?" asked the notary, pointing to the windshield.

"Why a bird?" asked my uncle.

"I'm a friend of the mill's owner," the notary said.

"Have you had many interested parties?"

"You're the first."

"Tell me, this mill . . . It is in the middle of the countryside, isn't it?"

"Totally isolated."

"And there's a river, and grass?" asked Uncle Alex, enchanted.

"Of course."

"And willows on the riverbank?"

"No. But there are quite a number of different trees."

"Tell me . . . this is a stupid question . . . I feel silly even asking . . ."

"Please, ask away," the notary said in a very gentle voice.

"It's a long-standing dream of mine . . . You know, there's that song . . . I'll try to sing it for you . . ."

This was the first time Uncle Alex had ever mentioned a song.

"These are the words . . ."

He hesitated as if he were about to let loose with an obscenity.

When next you see your river,
With the fields and woods all 'round . . .
And the crumbling bench near the old stone wall . . .

There was a moment of silence.

"Is the mill like in that song?" Uncle Alex finally asked.

"You'll see for yourself, sir."

We left the village and Uncle Alex had a hard time driving. I had to warn him when cars were approaching from the other direction. The notary showed us a road to the left; the moment we turned onto it, the windshield collapsed onto the dashboard in a shower of glass.

"It'll be easier to see this way," said Uncle Alex.

The notary pointed to a white wooden gate, with a wall on either side.

"Here it is, gentlemen."

We pushed open the gate, and I just had time to glimpse a wooden plaque on the right-hand wall that said, in faux-Chinese lettering, Yangtse Mill.

"Yangtse Mill?" I asked the notary.

"Yes."

He nodded, looking embarrassed.

"Why 'Yangtse'?" asked Uncle Alex, with an anxious face.

The notary didn't answer and then we were in the garden.

Farther on, in back, partly hidden by two copper beeches, I made out a kind of bungalow. As we went closer, I discovered it was built on stilts, and that its roof was composed of layered, upturned tiles. A large man with white hair was standing on the porch and waving at us. He came down the wooden steps and approached us with a supple gait. He wore a well-groomed chin beard that he kept stroking, and had big blue eyes.

"Monsieur Abott," the notary said, indicating the man.

"François Aubert and nephew," Uncle Alex said in a worldly voice.

"Pleased to meet you. If you'd care to come up . . ."

I glanced at Uncle Alex. He was very pale.

We walked up the steps to the porch. Abott and the notary went ahead.

"I thought . . . it was an old mill," my uncle said timidly.

"I knocked down the old mill five years ago and put this up instead," Abott stated. "It's much nicer. No comparison."

We remained motionless on the porch, my uncle and I, facing the other two. Abott grazed his chin beard with a cautious index finger. I don't know why, but I've never trusted men with overly groomed chin beards.

"It has much more character than the old mill, believe me," said the notary.

"Are you sure about that?" asked my uncle. He had grown even paler, and I was afraid he was going to faint.

"My friend Abott spent many years in Indochina," the notary said. "He's only been back since 1954, and he built this house so as not to feel too homesick. Personally, I find it has a ton of character . . . You *were* looking for something unusual, weren't you?"

"Not exactly," my uncle said.

Abott and the notary dragged us inside, into a long, narrow space, no doubt the living room.

"You will notice," the notary began sententiously, "that all the walls and partitions are made of genuine teak."

"All of them," Abott repeated. "Every one."

A stone bust of Buddha occupied a large niche facing us. On the walls were damaged paintings on silk, which seemed to bear traces of soot. Rocking chairs were arranged around a very low Chinese table with heavy corkscrew legs.

"What do you think?" I whispered to Uncle Alex.

He didn't hear. Looking grief-stricken, he pressed his lips together like someone about to cry in frustration.

"So?" asked Abott.

Uncle Alex kept silent. He crossed the room like an automaton, hunched over. He was having trouble forging a path amid all the Far Eastern knickknacks arranged in total disorder, the opium trays and rosewood screens. He stopped in front of a lacquer panel.

"That," said Abott, "is not just some piece of junk, I'll have you know. It's from the eighteenth century. It depicts the arrival of Louis XV's ambassadors at the Thai court in 1726."

"Are you selling that with the rest, Michel?" asked the notary.

"Depends on the price."

"I'm going to show the gentleman the other rooms."

"No," whispered my Uncle Alex. "There's no need . . ."

"But of course there is! Why not?" the notary exclaimed.

"No. No. Please . . ."

I lowered my eyes, expecting an outburst. I stared at the tips of my shoes and, a bit farther away, at a leopard skin of impressive dimensions splayed over the floor.

"Are you feeling all right?" asked Abott.

"It's nothing . . . I just need some air," Uncle Alex murmured.

We followed him out to the porch.

"Take a seat," said Abott, pointing to some rattan chairs.

Uncle Alex collapsed onto one of them. The notary and I sat down across from him.

"I'll fetch us some cool drinks," Abott said. "Please excuse me a moment . . ."

He disappeared into the living room. I caught his gesture of complicity for the notary, which seemed to say, Try to convince him—but perhaps I had a suspicious mind.

Regardless, that man with the well-groomed chin beard had seemed dubious from the outset. I could easily imagine him involved in some kind of currency smuggling.

"This is not at all what I expected," my uncle said in a moribund voice.

"Oh, no?"

"I thought it was a real mill, you understand . . ."

"This is just as good as a real mill, don't you think?" said the notary.

"It depends on your point of view . . . I want something restful, you understand . . ."

"But the Yangtse Mill is *utterly* restful," said the notary. "You'll feel like you're far from everything, thousands of miles away. Like being in a foreign country."

"I'm not looking for a foreign country," Uncle Alex replied gravely. "Besides, foreign from where?"

He suddenly fell silent, exhausted by that declaration.

"You should reconsider," said the notary. "It's a once-in-a-lifetime opportunity . . . Abott has some pressing obligations . . . He'd let you have it for a song . . . You ought to leap on the chance."

We remained silent. I tapped on a curious wooden table, small and circular.

"Do you know what that's called?" said the notary, nodding at the table.

"No."

"The Thai call it a rain drum."

Uncle Alex remained prostrate. A deluge began to fall, a tropical downpour, a monsoon.

"Speaking of rain," the notary said jokingly.

From the other end of the porch, a young Annamite, looking

like a domestic in his white jacket, came toward us carrying a tray. The rain redoubled in violence and the air felt very heavy. Uncle Alex mopped his brow. Abott reappeared, wearing a half-open khaki shirt. He stroked his beard.

"Here, I've brought you some quinine. Better safe than sorry," he said to Uncle Alex.

The domestic set the tray of refreshments down on the floor and Abott gave him an order, using the language of over there. The other lit a Chinese lantern that swung above our heads. At that moment, all the sadness and disappointment I had sensed in my uncle flooded over me as well. Throughout our trip, he had been dreaming of an old stone mill, with a river running through the grass, in the French countryside. We had driven through the Oise, the Orne, the Eure, and other regions. Finally, we had arrived in this village. But, Uncle, what good had all these efforts done us?

XII

Foucré was murmuring to someone near the window. A young blonde was sitting on the sofa, the only furnishing in the room. She was smoking. When I entered, Foucré turned. He came toward me, indicating the young woman:

"Let me introduce you to Denise Dressel."

I shook her hand and she gave me a distracted glance. Foucré had resumed his confabulation. I sat at the foot of the sofa while she ignored me.

I repeated to myself the name he had just spoken, Dressel, and immediately a first name appended itself to it in my mind: Harry. But who was Harry Dressel? I labored to put a face to those four syllables, whose combination seemed self-evident. I closed my eyes, the better to concentrate. Had someone once spoken to me of a certain Harry Dressel? Had I read that name somewhere? Had I met the man in some previous life? I heard myself asking in a toneless voice:

"Are you the daughter of Harry Dressel?"

She stared at me, then made a sudden movement and dropped her cigarette.

"How did you know?"

I searched for an answer. In vain. The question had occurred spontaneously and I would have liked to tell her so, but such a change had come over her face that I remained mute.

"Do you know Harry Dressel?"

She had said "Harry Dressel" almost in a whisper, as if the name burned her lips.

"A little, yes."

"That's impossible."

"I've heard a lot about him," I said, watching for any indication that would clue me in as to who this Harry Dressel actually was.

"People have talked to you about my father?" she asked anxiously.

"Lots of people."

"Why? Are you in show business?"

I saw a circus ring, heard the endless drumroll, while, far above, a trapeze artist is about to perform the salto mortale and, my eyes glued to the tips of my shoes, I pray for her safety.

"He was a great artist," I said.

She looked at me with gratitude. She had even taken my hand.

"Do you think people still remember him?"

"Of course."

"He would be so happy to hear that," she said.

I walked her home that evening. She wanted to show me a picture of her father, the only photo she had of him. As we walked, I stole glances at her. How old was she? Twenty-three. And I, barely seventeen. She was of average height, blonde, with pale, slanted eyes, a small nose, and carmine lips. Her cheekbones, bangs, and white fox-fur coat made her look Mongolian.

She lived in a cluster of buildings on Avenue Malakoff. We went through the vestibule and into her room. It was very spacious. Two French windows, a chandelier. The bed, wider than I'd ever seen, was covered with a leopard-skin throw. At the other end of the room, near one of the windows, a vanity in sky-blue satin. And side by side, on the back wall, two large photos in identical gilded frames. She immediately went to take them down and lay them on the bed.

The two faces had been captured in three-quarter view, heads slightly tilted. Underneath the photo of the man was his name in white letters: HARRY DRESSEL.

He seemed to be no more than thirty, with wavy blond hair, bright eyes, and a smile. He was wearing an open-throated shirt over a casually knotted polka-dot neckerchief. Between his portrait and his daughter's was probably a distance of more than twenty years, making father and daughter look more like brother and sister. It moved me to think that she had insisted on being photographed in the same pose and in the same lighting as her father.

"I look just like him, don't I? I'm every inch a Dressel."

She said "a Dressel" the way she might have said "a Hapsburg."

"If I'd wanted, I could have been in show business, too, but he wouldn't have liked that. And he would have been a hard act to follow."

"I'll bet he was a good father," I said.

She stared at me in surprise and delight. Finally, she had met somebody who understood that she was not the daughter of just anyone, but of Harry Dressel. Later, when I moved in with her, I foresaw that I'd play an important part in her life. I was the first person with whom she'd been able to talk about her father. And for her, that was the only topic of interest. I told her that her father fascinated me and that, since meeting him, I couldn't stop wondering about the man. I confided that I planned to write a biography of Harry Dressel. I would have done anything for her.

She hadn't seen him since 1951, back when she was still a child, for that was the year he'd been offered a job in Egypt, as emcee in a cabaret right near the Auberge des Pyramides. And then, in January 1952, the Cairo fire had, alas, coincided with the disappearance of Harry Dressel. He'd been living at the time in a hotel that burned to the ground. At least, that's what they'd said, but she didn't believe it.

She was convinced that her father was still alive, that he was hiding out for reasons of his own, but that someday he would resurface. I swore to her that I believed so too. Strange girl. She spent most of the afternoon stretched out on the large bed, in a bright red bathrobe, smoking cigarettes with an opiate aroma. And she always listened to the same records, which she asked me to put on ten or twenty times in a row. Rimsky-Korsakov's *Scheherazade* and a 78 whose grooves contained the overture of an operetta called *Deux sous de fleurs*.

At first, I couldn't fathom why she had so much money. I had seen her buy, on the same afternoon, a panther coat and several pieces of jewelry. She kindly offered to have suits made for me by a tailor whose clientele had included the dukes of Spoleto and Aosta, but I hadn't dared cross the threshold of that temple. I finally confessed that I wasn't very interested in clothes, and as she insisted on knowing what did "interest me," I said books. And to this day, I've kept the ones she was nice enough to give me: the six-volume Larousse encyclopedia; the complete Littré dictionary; Buffon's *Natural History*, in a very old, very handsomely illustrated deluxe edition; and finally, the *Memoirs* of Prince von Bülow, bound in pale green morocco leather. I was hurt when she explained to me, after a time, that she was being "kept" by an Argentinian who came to France every May to watch the polo championships in which his nephew competed. Yes, I was jealous of that Sr. Roberto Lorraine, whose photo she showed me: a short, pudgy man with gleaming black hair.

As for me, I was ready to start the book that would trace the life of her father, with all the passion I could muster. She was impatient to see me write the first pages. She wanted the setting to be worthy of such an enterprise, and thought long and hard about the table on which I would compose my opus.

She finally opted for an Empire desk overloaded with bronze fixtures. The chair on which I'd sit had arms covered in deep red velvet bordered by gold tacks, and a tall, solid back. Finally, I had to tell her it was hard for me to stay seated very long and she acquired a cathedral lectern that cost her a fortune. At such moments, I felt she loved me.

And there I was, that first evening, seated at my desk. On it were pencils she had sharpened. Two or three of those huge American-made fountain pens with full bladders. And bottles of ink in every hue. And erasers. And pink and green blotters. And a pad of letter-size writing paper open to a blank page. I wrote in block capitals: THE LIFE OF HARRY DRESSEL, and in the upper right-hand corner of the following page, the number 1. I had to start at the beginning, ask her what memories she had kept of her father, everything she knew about his childhood and youth.

Harry Dressel was born in Amsterdam. He had lost his parents at a very young age and left Holland for Paris. She couldn't say how he occupied his time until he reappeared in 1937, on the stage of the Casino de Paris, as one of Mistinguett's chorus boys.

The following year, he was hired by the Bagdad on Rue Paul-Cézanne to do a little variety number. The war caught him there. Afterward, he became, not exactly a star, but a top attraction. First at the Vol de Nuit until 1943. Then at the Cinq à Neuf until 1951, the date of his departure for Egypt, where he vanished. That, in broad strokes, was his professional career.

Denise's mother was one of those riders at the Bal Tabarin who sat astride the wooden horses of the carousel. The carousel turned and turned, ever more slowly, the horses reared, and the riders arched backward, breasts bare and hair loose. The orchestra played Weber's *Invitation to the Dance*. Dressel had lived with that girl for three years before she absconded to America. After that, he had raised Denise on his own.

One Sunday afternoon, she took me to the 18th arrondissement, to Square Carpeaux, where she and her father had lived. The windows of their small ground-floor apartment looked out on the park, so he could keep an eye on her while she played in the sandbox. That Sunday, the windows to the apartment were open. We heard people talking, but didn't dare peer inside. The sandbox hadn't changed a bit, she told me. And she relived the color and dusty aroma of the late Sunday afternoons she had experienced there. One Thursday, for her birthday, her father had taken her to a restaurant. She hadn't forgotten the route. You follow Rue Caulaincourt, beneath the acacias. The Mont-

martre of our childhood. A restaurant on the left, on the corner of Rue
Francoeur. It was there. For dessert, she had had strawberry-pistachio
ice cream. I noted all these details.

Her father got up very late. He told her he worked nights. When
he wasn't there, an older Flemish woman looked after her. And then,
he started talking about his departure for Egypt. The plan was for her
to come join him there after a few months, with the Flemish woman.

Despite the notes I was gathering, I couldn't fill the gaps in his
life story. For instance, what had Harry Dressel been doing until
1937?

I intended to go to Amsterdam to pursue my research and I had
sent two Dutch newspapers a brief ad for the "Information Wanted"
column, with Dressel's photo. "Anyone with information about the
activities of the variety artist and singer Harry Dressel before 1937,
please write: P. Modiano, c/o Dressel, 123-bis Avenue Malakoff,
Paris." No reply. I placed another request in the classifieds of a major
Paris daily: "Anyone with detailed information, professional or otherwise, about the singer-variety artist Harry Dressel during his time
in Egypt, July 1951–Jan. 1952, or any details on his life, please call
urgently, P. Modiano, Malakoff-10-28."

This time someone came forward, a certain Georges Jansenne,
who had been, he said on the phone, Dressel's impresario in "the final
years." He had a nervous voice, and I made an appointment to see
him. He was distrustful. He asked if "this was a trap." He preferred to
meet in a public place, and suggested a café on Place Victor-Hugo. I
agreed to his conditions. The book, first and foremost.

I'd told him he would recognize me because I was six and a half
feet tall, and I saw someone wave to me from the back of the terrace
at the Scossa. I sat at his table. You could tell he had been very blond
and curly, but over time, his blond hair, eyes, and complexion had
faded. The man was translucent. He gave me an albino gaze.

"So, you're interested in Harry Dressel? What is it you want to
know?"

His voice was almost inaudible. It was as if it had traveled years and years to reach me, and that it belonged to someone no longer of this world.

"I know his daughter," I said.

"What daughter? Dressel never had a daughter . . ."

He gave me a washed-out smile.

"I'm pleased that a boy your age cares about Dressel . . . As for me . . ."

I leaned in closer, so feeble was his voice. A sigh.

"As for me, I'd long forgotten about him . . . But when I read his name in your want ad . . . it gave me a pang."

He laid a hand on my arm, a hand with very pale, very thin skin, through which I could make out his bones and the entire network of veins.

"The first time I met Dressel . . ."

"The first time you met Dressel," I repeated eagerly.

". . . was in 1942, in Aiglon . . . He was leaning against the bar . . . an archangel . . ."

"Is that true?" I said.

"What's it to you?"

"Do you have other memories of him?"

His face lit up with the shadow of a smile.

"When Harry went into a café, he always sat near the window, in the sun, to get a tan . . ."

"Is that true?"

"He also used some kind of product to make his hair even blonder."

Jansenne knit his brow.

"How silly . . . I can't remember the name of it . . ."

He suddenly looked exhausted. He fell silent. If he stayed silent, who else could tell me about Harry Dressel? How many people were there in Paris who could have said that a man named Harry Dressel had existed? Just him and me. And Denise.

"I'd so like to hear more about him," I said.

"It's all so far in the past . . . Oh, here . . . I remembered the name of the product Harry always put in his hair . . . Bright & Shine . . . That's it . . . It was Bright & Shine . . ."

Around us, customers were making the most of the first sunny afternoon in April. Young people, mainly. They were wearing light-weight clothing in the latest fashions. Today, those clothes seem out-moded as well, but that afternoon, it was Jansenne's outfit—a very long coat with padded shoulders and a frayed-looking flannel suit—that gave the impression, by comparison, of belonging to a bygone era. I thought that if Harry Dressel were to sit at our table, he might cut the same ghostly figure as Jansenne.

"I served as his impresario toward the end," Jansenne murmured. "At the time of his departure for Egypt . . ."

He didn't answer all my questions, but according to him, no one would ever get to the bottom of what happened in Egypt. He had a very precise idea on the subject, and as I kept prodding him, he insinuated that Dressel had been murdered. That timid confession was the last thing I was able to drag out of him. He advised me half-heartedly to talk to a certain Edmond Jahlan, who, during Dressel's time in Egypt, was in King Farouk's entourage. Later, I searched for that Edmond Jahlan. In vain. So where are you, Jahlan? Get in touch.

He ordered a peppermint cordial and stared straight ahead with vacant eyes.

"What was Harry Dressel's act like?"

"He sang, mister. He was also a tap dancer."

"What songs did he sing?"

He knit his brow, as if to recall the titles.

"German songs. He had a signature tune:

"*Caprio-len . . .*
"*Ca-prio-len . . .*
"*Capriolen . . .*"

He tried to find the melody and his voice cracked. Long ago. So long ago.

"And he lived in Square Carpeaux, is that right?" I asked.

He shrugged and said in an exasperated tone:

"No, sir. Boulevard de la Tour-Maubourg."

"Did you know he had a daughter?"

"No, now give it a rest . . . That's the second time you've said that . . . You're kind of a joker, aren't you?"

He squinted and looked at me, a grimace playing on his lips.

"He was too fond of men."

His voice frightened me.

"I believe that's everything . . . I have nothing more to tell you . . ."

He stood up. So did I. We walked next to each other on the sidewalk of Place Victor-Hugo.

"Why do you want to stir up the past?"

He planted himself in front of me, almost threateningly, with his worn-out face and coat, his faded hair, his albino eyes.

"Can't you just leave us alone once and for all? Can't you?"

He turned on his heel. I stood there and watched him head toward Avenue Bugeaud. He didn't look back. A vague human shape, a puff of steam that could dissipate at any moment. Capriolen.

It was a long-term project. I explained this to Denise, in the evenings when she ventured into my "study." First I had to gather material proofs of Harry Dressel's passage on this earth. And that would take time. Already, combing through a stack of old newspapers, I had come across an advertisement for the Vol de Nuit nightclub, Rue des Colonels-Renard, that mentioned him by name. At the bottom of the "entertainments" page of another newspaper, another ad, but written in tiny characters: "The singer Harry Dressel is currently appearing at the Cinq à Neuf, Rue de Ponthieu. Tea—Aperitifs at 5pm—Dinner—Show at 8:30. Open all night." I clipped these documents and pasted them into a large sketchbook. I studied them under a magnifying glass for hours, so much had I come to doubt Harry Dressel's very existence. I also drew up long lists of people who, if still alive, could possibly tell me about him. And that required collecting scores of old phone directories. But the phone numbers no longer answered and my letters came back stamped "Addressee Unknown."

Dressel had had a dog. Denise remembered a Labrador named Mektoub. One night, when the "passive defense" sirens began to wail, they went down to the cellar, the Flemish woman, Denise, and the dog. At the Cinq à Neuf on Rue de Ponthieu, at the same hour, Dressel was just starting his act. In the cellar, the lights had gone out and they heard the thunder of the bombs, getting closer and closer. No doubt it was during the bombing of La Chapelle station. Denise hugged the dog tight and he licked her cheek. His rough tongue calmed the little girl's terror.

She still recalled the afternoon when she and her father had bought the Labrador, in a kennel in Auteuil, on Rue de l'Yvette. I went back there. The owner of the kennel, a sentimental fellow, had kept copies of the pedigrees and a small identity photo of every dog he had sold over the past forty years. He showed me his archives, which filled a large room, and he found the pedigree and picture of the Labrador. It was born on a breeding farm in Saint-Lô, in 1938, and the names of its parents and four grandparents were mentioned. The kennel owner gave me copies of the pedigree and photo. We had a long conversation. He dreamed of creating a centralized filing system in which every dog would be listed at birth. He also would have liked to collect every document—photos, feature films and home movies, oral and written testimony—relating to missing dogs. His personal torment was to think of those thousands and thousands of dogs who died in total anonymity, without leaving any trace.

I pasted the Labrador's pedigree and photo into the sketchbook, amid the other ephemera relating to Harry Dressel. Little by little, I began writing my book, in fragments. I had settled on the title: "The Lives of Harry Dressel," as what Jansenne had said induced me to think that Dressel had actually led several parallel lives. I had no proof of this and my file was rather sparse, but I figured I'd let my imagination run with it. It would help me find the real Dressel. I had only to let my mind wander about the few elements I had gathered, like an archeologist who, faced with a statue that is three-quarters mutilated, mentally reconstructs it entire. I worked at night. During the day, Denise stayed with me. We got up at around seven in the evening. Under her red bathrobe, she had a scent that I've sometimes recognized fleetingly on a passerby. At such moments, I relive the bedroom in the gray light of late afternoon, the fluid, prolonged sound of cars on rainy days, her eyes with their glints of mauve, her mouth, and the magic of her pale buttocks. When we managed to get up earlier, we went for walks in the Bois de Boulogne, by way of the lakes or the Pré Catelan. We talked about the future. We would get a dog. Maybe we'd take a trip. Would I like her to cut her hair? She was going on a diet starting today because she had gained a pound. Later on, would I read her some of what I'd written? We went for dinner at a restaurant on Rue Malakoff, a large dining room with walls covered in wood paneling that needed a fresh coat of paint, as did the four dilapidated Corinthian columns standing in the corners. Silence. Amber light. I was always careful to choose a table for three, in case Harry Dressel, coming through the door . . .

At around midnight, I sat down at my desk, in front of the writing pad. I was overcome by fatigue the instant I uncapped my pen. My dear Dressel, how I've suffered because of you . . . But I don't hold it against you. I'm the guilty party. I'm certain you had doubts about your life, which would explain why I've found so few traces of it. And so I was forced to guess, to give a father to your daughter, whom I loved. From her bed in the next room, she would ask, "How's it coming along?" and put on a record of Rimsky-Korsakov because she believed that music helps you write more easily.

At the beginning of May, Sr. Roberto Lorraine, her protector, arrived from Argentina accompanied by his nephew and the latter's polo team. She told me we'd be seeing each other less often. I could continue to live at her place, and she would come visit me from time to time so that I could read her further installments of the book about her father. I worked all day long to console myself for her absence. I had written nearly fifty pages about Dressel's early years, a period of his life about which I knew nothing. I'd made him into a kind of David Copperfield, and I skillfully mixed a few passages of Dickens in with my prose. His teenage years in Amsterdam were imbued with an "atmosphere" that owed much to the late, lamented Francis Carco. But from the moment when Dressel began his artistic career at the Casino de Paris and met Denise's mother, I found a more personal tone.

His departure and time in Egypt in 1951 particularly inspired me, and my pen flew over the paper. Between Cairo and Alexandria, I was at home. The blue-and-gold nightclub where Dressel was master of ceremonies, near the Auberge des Pyramides, was called the Scarab, and the "artist" Annie Beryer appeared on its stage. King Farouk came to hear her sing and instructed his Italian secretary to bring Annie jewels of great value, but the secretary had copies made and kept the originals for himself. Other individuals haunted that establishment, survivors of who knows what shipwreck. And what about Harry Dressel? When was he last seen? In January, a few days before the fire, when Mme. Sazzly Bey had given a party to inaugurate her new mansion on the outskirts of Cairo, an exact copy of Tara from *Gone with the Wind*, with its cedar-lined driveway . . .

I read the chapters to Denise. She could no longer sleep with me on Avenue Malakoff. Sr. Roberto Lorraine had told her he wanted to marry her. He was thirty years older than she; she found him overweight and didn't like men who used cosmetics . . . But he was— apparently—one of the three richest men in Argentina. I was in despair, but I hid it from her.

She sometimes paid me a brief visit at around two in the morning. She had managed to slip out of the Eléphant Blanc, where

Sr. Roberto Lorraine and his nephew were waiting for daybreak. I showed her my latest pages and she never expressed any surprise at the twists and turns in the "lives of Harry Dressel."

We had a few more lazy afternoons. She wrapped herself in the leopard skin and I continued to read her the thousand and one adventures of her father.

One evening, I returned to Avenue Malakoff, my arms laden with three large reels that I'd sneaked out of the cinema archives with the help of an employee. It was the first part of a film shot in 1943, *The Wolf of the Malveneurs*, in which Dressel had had a walk-on part. I planned to rent a projector and copy one by one the frames in which he was recognizable.

All the lights in the apartment were on, but no one was home. On my Empire desk, a hastily scribbled note:

"I'm off to live in Argentina. Keep writing the book on Papa. Love, Denise."

I sat at the desk. I had set the three film reels on the floor, at my feet. I felt an emptiness that I had known since childhood, from the moment I'd understood that people and things will leave you someday, will disappear. As I walked through the rooms, the feeling grew stronger. The portraits of Dressel and his daughter were gone. Had she taken them to Argentina? The bed, the leopard skin, the blue satin vanity would furnish other rooms, other cities, or perhaps some closet, and soon no one would remain to know that these objects had been brought together, for a very brief time, in a bedroom on Avenue Malakoff, by the daughter of Harry Dressel.

Except for me. I was seventeen, and all that remained was for me to become a French writer.

XIII

At the end of the year, I got married. I spent the months preceding that remarkable ceremony with the woman who would become my wife, in Tunisia, her homeland. There, dusk doesn't exist. Doze off for just a minute on the terrace of Sidi-Bou-Saïd and night has fallen.

We left the house and its smell of jasmine. It was the hour when, at the Café des Nattes, Aloulou Cherif and his pals started dealing hands of *belote*. We walked down the road that leads to El Marsa and overlooks the sea, which in the early morning hours is enveloped in silver vapor. Then, little by little, it takes on the color of an ink I used to love when I was a child because we were forbidden to use it in school: aqua blue. One last bend, one last road bordered by villas, and, on the left, the local depot. Shadows waited for the train. A lamppost on the platform weakly illuminated the station, its white façade, the old awning with its metal lacework. That station might just as easily have been in Montargis or Saint-Lô if not for the blue of the awning and the white façade that gave it away.

Across the street, in the gentle breeze, people crushed in to drink pine nut tea or play dominos. We heard the murmur of conversations encouraged by the darkness. Now and again, the phosphorescent white of a djellaba. The movie theater was playing *Roman Holiday*, with, as second feature, an Arabic film starring Farid al Atrache. I own an old photo of that actor with his sister, the singer Asmahane. Both of them belonged to a princely family from Jabal al-Druze. The photo was given to me that year by an old barber in El Marsa whose shop was located in that street, to the right, after the theater. He had displayed it in his window, and I had been struck by the likeness between my wife and the strange Asmahane, who they said was both a singer and a spy.

We walked along the promenade by the sea, with its twin rows of palm trees. It was dark. Past the French embassy, we entered the residential quarter of El Marsa. We stopped at the crest of a street that heads down toward the water. We pushed open an iron gate and were in Borj, where my wife's family lived.

We followed a path above the sloping garden, with the sea in the distance. A short surrounding wall covered in bougainvillea supported a small gate. We passed through another gate and arrived at a kind of patio.

They were all there, sitting around garden tables, speaking in low voices or playing cards: Doctor Tahar Zaouch, Youssef Guellaty, Fatma, Mamia, Chefika, Jaouidah, and others I didn't know, faces half submerged in shadow. We sat down in turn and joined the conversation. In June, they had left Tunis and the regally sumptuous apartment on Rue de la Commission and settled in Borj for the summer. Every evening would be like this; we would come join them, chatting or playing cards around the table, in the blue light.

We walked down the garden steps with our dear friends Essia and Moncef Guellaty. At the bottom, a path marked the boundary of what had once been the estate of the Dutch painter Nardus: a large park stretching to the beach. They had split it into plots; a host of small houses, ringed by little gardens, replaced the shade trees of the park, where the blonde Flo, Nardus's daughter, used to wander nude, so long ago . . . The pink marble villa with its turret hadn't been demolished. When there was a full moon, we could make out Nardus's bust, sculpted by him, rising white and solitary in front of the villa. The new owners had left it intact. It faced toward us, its plaster eye fixed on the beach. All that remained of the park was a clump of eucalyptus trees that perfumed the night.

Often, after our visit to Borj, we would take the Gammarth road.

It ran alongside the sea. A little before Gammarth, we stopped in front of the Dunes inn.

A stairway. There was a terrace whose floor was made of marble with black-and-white diamond shapes. Most of the tables were sheltered by a trellis of foliage. We always chose the same one, on the edge of the terrace, from where we could see the beach and the sea.

We listened to the surf, and the wind brought me the last echoes of Alexandria and, farther still, those of Thessaloniki and of many other cities before they were burned down. I was about to marry the woman I loved and I was finally back in the Orient that we never should have left.

XIV

As I was leafing through a newspaper, my eyes fell on the real estate ads and I read:

"Empty. Apartment Quai Conti — River view — 4th floor. No elevator. Danton-55-61."

My hunch was confirmed when I phoned. Yes, it was indeed the same apartment where I'd spent my childhood. I don't know why, but I asked to see it.

The real estate agent, a fat, brilliantined redhead, preceded me up the stairs. On the fourth floor, he pulled a ring with about a dozen keys from his pocket and without any hesitation found the right one. He pushed open the front door and stepped aside:

"After you."

A pang in my heart. It had been more than fifteen years since I'd walked through that door. A light bulb hanging from a wire lit the vestibule, whose walls still retained their pinkish-beige tint. To the right, the rack where my father hung his many overcoats, and the shelving on which we stored — I still remember — several old valises and a canvas hat for warm climates. The brilliantined redhead opened one of the vestibule doors and we went into the entrance hall that served as our dining room. As it was barely 7 o'clock on that June evening, a soft amber light flooded the room. He gripped my arm:

"I'm terribly sorry . . ."

Sweat was dripping down his temples. He seemed very nervous.

"I . . . I left my briefcase at a client's house . . . Or at least . . . I hope it's there . . . I need to go right away . . . I'll only be fifteen minutes . . ."

His eyes were wide and he looked panic-stricken. What was in that briefcase to put him in such a state? What was he afraid of?

"Would you mind terribly waiting for me here?"

"Not at all."

"You can maybe start looking around the apartment."

"Of course."

He walked quickly to the vestibule.

"Back in a minute . . . Back in a minute . . . Have a look around."

The door slammed behind him.

I found myself alone, in the part of the room where the table stood at which we used to eat our meals. The sun sketched orange stripes on the wood floor. Not a sound. The oxeye window, through which you could see the bedroom, was still there. I remember where the furniture was placed. The two large world globes on either side of the window. Beneath it, the glassed-in bookcase supporting a model galleon. At the foot of the bookcase, a miniature reproduction of one of those cannons used in the Battle of Fontenoy. The two wooden mannequins with their armor and coat of mail, each behind one of the globes. And in front of the model galleon, the saber that had belonged to the Duke of Gloucester. Across the room, in a recess in the wall, was a sofa, and on either side of it were bookshelves: when I used to sit there before dinner and peruse one of the red cloth-covered volumes, I felt as if I was in a train compartment.

Empty, the room seemed smaller. Or was it my adult eyes bringing it down to size? I moved into the "summer dining room," a kind of wide corridor with black-and-white-tiled floor, and a bay window through which you could see the rooftops of the Monnaie de Paris and the garden of the neighboring house. The rectangular table with its faux-marble top appeared to me in ghostly superimposition. And the orange leather bench, faded by the sun. And the wallpaper, which depicted a scene from *Paul et Virginie*. I crossed back through the entrance hall toward the two rooms that overlooked the quay. Someone had ripped out the hallway mirror. I went into what had been my father's office, and there I felt a deep sadness. No more sofa, no more curtains whose matching fabric was decorated with dark red leaf patterns. No more portrait of Beethoven on the wall, at left, near the door. No more bust of Buffon in the center of the mantelpiece. Nor that scent of chypre and English tobacco.

Nothing left.

I climbed the small interior stairway to the fifth floor and entered the room on the right, which my father had turned into a bathroom. The black floor tiles, the fireplace, and the white marble bathtub were still there, but in the room facing the Seine, the sky-blue paneling had disappeared, and I stared at a bare wall. Here and there, it bore traces of wall fabric, remnants of the occupants before my parents, and it occurred to me that if I scraped away these bits of fabric, I'd discover minuscule fragments of still older layers.

It was nearly eight o'clock, and I began to wonder whether the brilliantined redhead from the agency had forgotten about me. The room was bathed in a dusky light that projected small golden rectangles on the back wall, just like twenty years ago. One of the windows was slightly ajar, and I leaned my elbows on the rail. Very little traffic. A few remaining fishermen at the tip of Ile de la Cité, beneath the heavy foliage of the Vert-Galant garden. A quayside bookseller, whom I recognized by his tall outline and cape—he was already there when I was a child—folded up his canvas chair and headed off slowly toward the Pont des Arts.

At fifteen, waking up in this room, I would pull open the curtains, and the sunlight, the Saturday strollers, the booksellers unlocking their stalls, the passage of a platform bus, all of it felt reassuring. A day like any other. The catastrophe I dreaded, without quite knowing what it was, had not occurred. I would go down into my father's office and read the morning papers. He, in his blue bathrobe, was making endless phone calls. He would ask me to come meet him, at the end of the afternoon, in some hotel lobby where he held his appointments. We dined at home. Afterward, we went to see an old film or have a sherbet, on summer evenings, on the sidewalk of the Ruc-Univers. Sometimes the two of us stayed in his office, listening to records or playing chess, and he would scratch the top of his scalp with his index finger before moving a pawn. He walked me to my room and smoked a last cigarette while telling me about his "projects."

And like the successive layers of paper and fabric that covered the walls, that apartment evoked still more distant memories: the several years that matter so deeply to me, even though they precede my birth. At the end of a day in June 1942, in a dusk as mild as today's, a pedicab stops, downstairs, in the narrow byway off Quai de Conti between the Monnaie and the Institut de France. A young woman gets out of the pedicab. It's my mother. She has just arrived in Paris on the train from Belgium.

I remembered that between the two windows, near the bookshelves, there was a writing desk whose drawers I would explore when I lived in that room. Among the old cigarette lighters, cheap necklaces, and keys that no longer opened any doors—what doors *had* they opened?—I had come across small datebooks from the years 1942, 1943, and 1944, which belonged to my mother and which I've since misplaced. Having leafed through them so often, I knew by heart all the brief notes she had jotted in there. Such as, one day in the autumn of 1942: "Toddie Werner's—Rue Scheffer."

It was there that she first met my father. A girlfriend had dragged her to that apartment on Rue Scheffer, occupied by two young women: Toddie Werner, a German Jew living there under an assumed identity, and her friend, a certain Liselotte, also German, married to an Englishman whom she was trying to free from the camp in Saint-Denis. That evening, about a dozen guests were gathered on Rue Scheffer. They talked, listened to music, and the drawn curtains required by "passive defense" made for an even more intimate mood. My mother and father were talking. Everyone who was there with them, and who could have borne witness to their first meeting and to that evening, is now gone.

Leaving Rue Scheffer, my father and Geza Pellmont wanted to go visit Koromindé on Rue de la Pompe. They invited my mother along. They climbed into Pellmont's Ford. He was a Swiss citizen and had obtained a travel pass. My father often said that when he sat in Pellmont's Ford, he had the illusion he couldn't be touched by the Gestapo or the inspectors from Rue Greffulhe, because that car was, in a sense, a bit of Swiss territory. But the Milice requisitioned it not long afterward, and it was in that Ford that they assassinated Georges Mandel.

At Koromindé's, they let the curfew hour slide by, and they stayed there, chatting, until dawn.

In the following weeks, my father and mother got to know each other better. They often arranged to meet in a small Russian restaurant on Rue Faustin-Hélie. At first, he didn't dare tell my mother that he was Jewish. Since arriving in Paris, she had been working for the dubbing department of Continental Films, a German production company located on the Champs-Elysées. He was hiding out in a riding academy in the Bois de Boulogne, where the instructor was a childhood friend of his.

Yesterday, we walked, my little daughter and I, in the Jardin d'Acclimatation, and by chance we arrived at the edge of that riding academy. Thirty-three years had passed. The brick buildings of the stables where my father took refuge had surely not changed since then, nor had the hurdles, the white barriers, the black sand of the bridle path. Why here, more than any other place, did I smell the venomous odor of the Occupation, the compost from which I emerged?

Troubled times. Unexpected encounters. By what twist of fate did my parents spend New Year's Eve 1942 at the Beaulieu, in the company of the actor Sessue Hayakawa and his wife, Flo Nardus? A photo lay at the bottom of the drawer in the writing desk, which showed the four of them seated at a table, Sessue Hayakawa, as stone-faced as in *Gambling Hell*; Flo Nardus, so blonde that her hair looks white; my mother and father, looking like two timid youngsters . . . That evening, Lucienne Boyer was headlining at the Beaulieu, and just before they announced the New Year, she sang a song forbidden because one of its composers was Jewish:

> *Speak to me of love*
> *Tell me again*
> *Those tender words . . .*

Sessue Hayakawa has since passed away. What was that Japanese former Hollywood star doing in Paris under the Occupation? He and Flo Nardus lived at 14 Rue Chalgrin in a small house at the back of a courtyard, where my father and mother often visited. Nearby, on Rue Le Sueur—the first street on the right—Dr. Petiot was incinerating the bodies of his victims. In the ground-floor studio, with its twisted columns, dark paneling, and cathedras, Sessue Hayakawa greeted my parents in a "battle" kimono. Flo Nardus's blondness was even more unreal next to that samurai. She tended to the complicated flowers and plants that gradually invaded the studio. She also raised lizards. She had spent her childhood and adolescence in Tunisia, at El Marsa, in a pink marble villa owned by her father, a Dutch painter. And it was in Tunisia that I met her in July 1976. I'd learned that she had settled in that country some time before, like people who return to their birthplace.

I called her on the phone and told her my name. After more than thirty years, she still remembered my parents. We set a date for Thursday, July 8, at 6 p.m., at the Tunisia Palace on Avenue de Carthage.

The hotel must have had its heyday under the Protectorate, but now the lobby, with its few chairs and bare walls, looked abandoned. Near me sat a fat man in a very tight black suit who jiggled an amber necklace in his right hand. Someone came to greet him, calling him Hadji.

I thought about my parents. I was certain that, if I wanted to meet witnesses and friends from their youth, it would always be in places like this: disused hotel lobbies in far-off countries, over which floated a scent of exile, harboring creatures who had never had a home base or defined civil status. While waiting for Flo Nardus, I felt the gentle, furtive presence of my father and mother next to me. I saw her enter and recognized her immediately. I stood up and waved. She was wearing a pink turban, a blouse of the same color, slacks, and tattered espadrilles. Around her waist was a belt made of bits of orange glass and shards of mirror strung together with silver wire. She was still the woman in the photo. Her profile was very smooth and her eyes forget-me-not blue.

I surprised her by talking about the past. She herself didn't recall too many details. Then, little by little, her memory cleared and it was as if she were giving me back a very old magnetic tape that had been forgotten in a drawer.

She remembered that my father had hidden for a month at 14 Rue Chalgrin, not daring to leave the house because he had no papers and was afraid of roundups. Sessue Hayakawa's papers weren't in order, either. The Germans didn't know that this Japanese had an American passport, and the Japanese wanted to draft him. In the evening, my father, Sessue, and she played dominos to take their minds off their troubles, or else my father helped Sessue rehearse his role in *Patrouille Blanche*, a film he was in, directed by Christian Chamborant. My father was an old friend. He had been a witness at her and Sessue's wedding, in 1940, at the Japanese consulate. Yes, she recalled that evening at the Beaulieu, but they had gotten together a week before that, at 14 Rue Chalgrin, to celebrate Christmas: my father, my mother, Toddie Werner, Korominde, Pellmont, all the others . . .

We were the only ones left in the lobby. The sounds of cars and horns drifted in from the street, and we sat there, talking about a past that had brought us together but that was so far distant it had lost all reality.

We left the hotel and followed Avenue Bourguiba. Night was falling. Hundreds of birds hidden in the leaves of the trees on the median strip cheeped in a deafening concert. I leaned closer to hear what she was saying. In the past thirty years, she had known her share of hardships. They had arrested her at the Liberation, accusing her of being a "Kraut spy," but she had managed to escape from Tourelles prison. Already during the Phony War, when she and Hayakawa lived on Rue de Saussure, in the Batignolles neighborhood, the locals accused them of being "Fifth Columnists."

Sessue had returned to America. He had died. She had lost her father. They had impounded her childhood villa in El Marsa. She lived in a room in the Medina, and to get by she made little glass animals: reptiles, fish, birds. Painstaking work. She cut pieces of glass, fitted them together, and bound them with wire. Someday, if I liked, she would show me her animals. We'd have to meet earlier and we'd walk to her home on Rue Sidi-Zahmoul. But this evening it was too late, and I'd risk getting lost on the way back. I accompanied her to Porte de France. She walked down one of the alleys with an indolent, graceful step and I gazed after her silhouette amid the cloth, perfume, and jewelry merchants taking down their stalls. She waved to me one last time before being lost in the crowd of souks. With her, it was a bit of my parents' youth drifting away.

I've kept a photo of such small dimensions that I scrutinize it under a loupe to see the details. They're sitting side by side, on the living room sofa, my mother with a book in her right hand, her left hand resting on my father's shoulder as he leans forward to pet a large black dog whose breed I can't make out. My mother is wearing a curious striped blouse with long sleeves; her blond hair falls to her shoulders. My father is wearing a light-colored suit. With his brown hair and pencil mustache, he looks like the American aviator Howard Hughes. Who could have taken that picture, one evening during the Occupation? Without that period, and the random, incongruous meetings it brought about, I would never have been born. Evenings when my mother, in the fifth-floor bedroom, read or looked out the window. Downstairs, the front door closed with a metallic thud. It was my father returning from his obscure errands. The two of them dined together, in the summer dining room on the fourth floor. Then they went into the living room, which served as my father's office. There, they had to shut the curtains, because of passive defense. They listened to the radio, probably, and my mother clumsily typed up the subtitles she had to deliver to Continental Films every week. My father read *Bodies and Souls* by Van der Meersch or the *Memoirs* of Prince von Bülow. They talked, made plans. Often laughed uproariously.

One evening, they had gone to the Mathurins to see a drama called *Solness the Builder* and had run out of the theater doubled over. They couldn't contain their laughter. They howled with laughter all the way down the sidewalk, right near Rue Greffulhe, where policemen stood who wanted my father dead. Sometimes, when they had drawn the curtains in the living room and the silence was so complete that they could hear a carriage passing by or the rustle of trees on the quay, I imagine my father felt a vague disquiet. Fear overcame him, like on one late afternoon in the summer of '43. There was a downpour and he was beneath the arcades of Rue de Rivoli. People waited in compact groups for the rain to stop. And the arcades grew darker and darker. A climate of expectancy, of suspended movement, the kind that preceded police roundups. He didn't dare mention his anxiety. He and my mother were two rootless souls, with no attachments of any kind; two butterflies in the darkness of Occupied Paris, when one could so easily pass from shadows to too harsh a light, and from light to shadow. One day, at dawn, the telephone rang and an unknown voice asked for my father by his real name. They hung up immediately. That was the day he decided to flee Paris . . . I had sat down between the two windows, at the foot of the shelving. Darkness had invaded the room. Back then, the telephone used to be on the writing desk, easily at hand. It seemed, after thirty years, that I could still hear that shrill, half-muffled ringing.

I still hear it.

The front door slammed. Footsteps on the interior stairs. Someone came closer.

"Where are you? Are you there?"

The real estate man, the brilliantined redhead . . . I recognized the effluvia of Roja that he left in his wake.

I stood up. He stretched out his hand.

"Forgive me. I was gone a long time."

He was relieved. He had found his briefcase. He joined me at one of the windows.

"Were you able to look around the apartment? You can't see a thing now. I should have brought a flashlight."

At that instant, the tour boat appeared. It glided toward the tip of the island, its garland of searchlights aimed at the building façades along the quays. The walls of the room were suddenly covered in spots, dots of light, lattice patterns that spun around and vanished into the ceiling. In that same room, twenty years earlier, the same fleeting, familiar shadows had captivated my brother Rudy and me, when we turned off our lamp as the same boat passed by.

They must have been celebrating something that evening. The Louvre, the Vert-Galant garden, and the statue of Henri IV on the Pont-Neuf were all lit up.

"What do you think of that view?" the brilliantined redhead asked, in a faint but triumphant voice. "It's really something, isn't it? Eh?"

I didn't know what to answer. In 1945, one evening in May, the quays and the Louvre were lit up just like this. A crowd had swarmed onto the banks of the Seine and the Vert-Galant garden. Below, in the byway off Quai de Conti, a dance party had spontaneously broken out.

They played the "Marseillaise" and the "Valse brune." My mother, leaning on the balcony, watched the people dancing. I would be born in July. My father, too, was somewhere amid that crowd celebrating the first night of peace. The day before, he had left on a train with Pellmont, as they had discovered the Ford in the back of a shed, near Narbonne. The back seat was smeared with blood.

A taxi was parked at the corner of Rue Gambetta and Rue de France. I hesitated before opening the door because a man was sitting next to the driver, but he nodded that the car was free.

My wife and I took seats in back, and in my arms I carried my daughter, who had just turned one year old. I was thirty and four months, and my wife would soon be twenty-five.

We placed the navy-blue stroller between us. The man sitting in front, to the driver's right, didn't move. I finally said:

"We're going to Cimiez, the Arenas."

The driver started up slowly. He was a fellow about my age, as was his neighbor.

"Problem with the distributor . . ."

"Even in a diesel?"

"I should go see your brother . . ."

"He's not at the Greuze garage anymore."

They both spoke with a Nice accent. The one driving had turned on the radio, low. My wife was now holding the baby, showing her the fronts of the houses parading by outside the window.

The driver, a blond, had a wispy mustache. His friend was dark and stocky; his eyes, sunk deep in their sockets, made his face look like an ancient ram.

"Did you hear they're going to knock down Greuze?"

"How come?"

"Ask Gabizon."

The baby was playing with my wife's necklace. She shook it and put it in her mouth. We followed Boulevard Victor-Hugo between rows of plane trees. Monday, December 1, 1975, at two in the afternoon. Sunny.

We turned left onto Rue Gounod and drove past the hotel of the same name, a white edifice whose revolving door was closed. I just had time to spot behind a fence a narrow garden that might have turned into a park, all the way in back. And suddenly, it seemed to me that in another life, one summer evening, I had passed through that revolving door, while music drifted from the garden. Yes, I had stayed in that hotel. I retained a vague recollection and the odd impression that in those days, I had a wife and a little girl, the same ones as today. How could I pick up the traces of that former life?

I would have had to consult the old registration cards of the Gounod Hotel. But what was my name back then? And where were the three of us coming from?

"Yes, yes, it's Gabizon . . ."

"You surprised?"

"He pulled the same thing with the Porsche dealership."

"Exactly."

The dark-haired man with the ram's head lit a cigarillo, dragging on it in nervous puffs. He turned toward us.

"Oh, forgive me . . . The baby . . ."

He pointed with a smile to the cigarillo, which he stubbed out in the ashtray.

"Smoke is bad for infants," he said to us.

I was amazed by such delicacy and concluded that he, too, must have a child.

I don't know why we took this detour, but we followed Boulevard du Parc-Impérial, leaving the Russian church behind us. There was probably an old man dozing in its shade who long ago had been one of the czarina's pages. We arrived at the top of Boulevard de Cimiez and the baby looked out the window. It was the first time she'd gone through Nice in a car. Everything she was seeing was new to her, the green smudge of the trees, the automobile traffic, the pedestrians on the sidewalks.

"And your brother?"

"No sweat, he's got it covered . . ."

"With the old Facel Vegas?"

"Of course, Patrick . . ."

So the dark-haired man with the ram's head had the same name as me, a name that had been in vogue in 1945, perhaps because of the English-speaking soldiers, the jeeps, and the first American bars opening. The entire year 1945 was contained in the two syllables of "Patrick." We, too, had once been infants.

"There's not only the Facels . . ."

"Oh?"

"He also picked up more than a dozen Nashes."

What was Nice like in 1945? Strains of jazz filtered through the windows of the Ruhl Hotel, commandeered by the American army. My poor sister Corinne, whom the French military police had arrested in Italy, was locked up right nearby, in Villa Saint-Anne, before being taken to prison, then to the Pasteur Hospital . . . And in Paris, the survivors of the camps waited in striped pajamas, beneath the chandeliers of the Hotel Lutétia.

I remember all of it. I peel away the bills posted in successive layers for the past fifty years until I reach the earliest scraps. We passed by what had been the Winter-Palace and I saw the young English-women and young tubercular Russians in 1910. The taxi slowed down, came to a stop. We had arrived at the garden of the Arenas. The dark fellow with the ram's head, the one named Patrick, got out and helped us remove the stroller, a very complicated model with six wheels, adjustable pivoting seat, collapsible canopy, and mobile steel handlebar, to which one could attach an umbrella. He waved to us as the taxi pulled away.

I had taken my daughter in my arms and she was asleep, her head resting on my shoulder. Nothing troubled her slumber.

She didn't yet have any memory.

PATRICK MODIANO, winner of the 2014 Nobel Prize in Literature, was born in Boulogne-Billancourt, France, in 1945, and published his first novel, *La Place de l'Etoile*, in 1968. In 1978 he was awarded the Prix Goncourt for *Rue des Boutiques Obscures* (published in English as *Missing Person*), and in 1996 he received the Grand Prix National des Lettres for his body of work. Modiano's other writings in English translation include *Suspended Sentences*, *Pedigree: A Memoir*, *After the Circus*, *Paris Nocturne*, *Little Jewel*, *Sundays in August*, *Such Fine Boys*, and *Sleep of Memory* (all published by Yale University Press), as well as the memoir *Dora Bruder*, the screenplay *Lacombe, Lucien*, and the novels *So You Don't Get Lost in the Neighborhood*, *Young Once*, *In the Café of Lost Youth*, and *The Black Notebook*.

MARK POLIZZOTTI has translated more than fifty books from the French, including works by Gustave Flaubert, Marguerite Duras, Jean Echenoz, Raymond Roussel, and eight other volumes by Patrick Modiano. A Chevalier of the Ordre des Arts et des Lettres and the recipient of a 2016 American Academy of Arts and Letters Award for Literature, he is the author of eleven books, including *Revolution of the Mind: The Life of André Breton*, which was a finalist for the PEN/ Martha Albrand Award for First Nonfiction; *Luis Buñuel's Los Olvidados*; *Bob Dylan: Highway 61 Revisited*; and *Sympathy for the Traitor: A Translation Manifesto*. His essays and reviews have appeared in the *New York Times*, the *New Republic*, the *Wall Street Journal*, *ARTnews*, the *Nation*, *Parnassus*, *Bookforum*, and elsewhere. He directs the publications program at The Metropolitan Museum of Art in New York.